Acclaim for LAWRENCE SHAINBERG

Brain Surgeon: An Intimate View of His World

"The author's knowledge of the brain and the craft of neurosurgery . . . is so profound for a layman as to verge on the unbelievable."

—*The New York Times Book Review*

Memories of Amnesia

"By writing a novel from the brain's point of view, Mr. Shainberg bravely assumes the novelists' liabilities, and, mostly, surmounts them by his bold fictional strategy. It would be nice to report that, having pinpointed philosophical questions central to many issues in modern life, Dr. Drogin (or Mr. Shainberg) had also resolved them, but of course that would be far beyond the responsibility of a novelist (or neurosurgeon). In engaging them at all, he has produced a distinctive, absorbing, and amusing work."

—*The New York Times*

Ambivalent Zen

"Though it touches on psychic sufferings, crippling indecision, and the intense physical pain of sitting cross-legged and motionless for long spans of time, *Ambivalent Zen* is so user-friendly and affable that it's easy to forget how hard the book must have been to write. Though Shainberg has trouble with his meditation posture, he keeps his literary balance nicely."

—Francine Prose, *Newsday*

Crust

a novel by
LAWRENCE SHAINBERG

For Rose,
with great appreciation
for your help, not
to mention your cookies.

Love,
Larry
9/8/08

TWO DOLLAR RADIO
Since*2005

Published by the Two Dollar Radio Movement, 2008.
Copyright 2008 by Lawrence Shainberg.

ISBN: 978-0-9763895-8-3
LCCN: 2008932451

Visit these websites:
nasalism.blogspot.com
LawrenceShainberg.com

All rights reserved. Used by permission:
Illustrations by Michael Flanagan;
20 Beth Jones, photo by Michael Flanagan;
83 Lovie LeFlore;
88 "Pick It," Erica Simone Leeds;
91 Special thanks to Barbara Kruger;
116 "Homeland Security Helmet," Bob Pagani;
126 Stephen Jaffe/Getty Images;
184 Dave, photo by Andrew David Francis.

Distributed to the trade by **Consortium Book Sales & Distribution, Inc.**
34 Thirteenth Avenue NE, Suite 101
Minneapolis, Minnesota 55413-1007
www.cbsd.com
phone 612.746.2600 | fax 612.746.2606
orders 800.283.3572

Two Dollar Radio
Book publishers since 2005.
"Because we make more noise than a $2 radio."
www.TwoDollarRadio.com
twodollar@TwoDollarRadio.com

For Norman Mailer

"Everything that man handles has a tendency to secrete meaning."

—Marcel Duchamp

"… excrement is a representation of death that we ourselves produce and that, indeed, we cannot help producing in the very process of maintaining our lives. Perhaps it is for making death so intimate that we find excrement so repulsive."

—Harry G. Frankfurt

Crust

The crust was there when I woke up. Such was its insistence that it seemed I'd never known one before. It was large and dense and high in my right nostril, attached to the septum as well as the upper lateral cartilage, thus perfectly situated to activate the trigeminal nerve through which, as most research confirms, the chaos of sensation it generated was being transmitted to anterior cells in my hippocampus[1] or, if you prefer (as I do) Robert Fawck's contrarian view of this neurology, the dorsal cells of my frontal insula.[2] Lucille Bloch's classification scale (**Appendix A**)[3] was still two years away from publication, and I'd not yet discovered the website on which she was already publishing data, but had I been familiar with her work, I'd have recognized this crust at once as an 8 or an 8.5, with the potential to become a 9 or even a 10 since the radiators in our bedroom were, as usual, generating too much heat and we'd yet to purchase the humidifier we'd promised ourselves for years.[4] Like any 8, it was in all probability more

1 Karshman, Anselm. *Nasal Neurology* (Berkeley: University of California Press, 2009) 12–67.

2 Fawck, Robert. "Essential Nasalism," *Scientific American* June 2010: 58–73.

3 Bloch, Lucille. *Nasal Classification* (New York: Murgate, 2012). See also Bloch's blog, Crustclassification.com, which was already fourteen months old at this point in time.

4 See Humidifier.com or G.E./humidifier.net for a summary of recent research on the interrelationship of nasal obstruction and humidity.

than .2 but less than .6 millimeters in diameter and between 2 and 3 cubic centimeters in volume. The effects of extraction

Figure 1   Lucille Bloch.

are always hard to predict, of course (even Bloch, **Figure 1**, is reticent here), but it was more than likely that, in the immediate aftermath of its emergence, its shape and color would be similar to, though not identical with, *Plate 43* in the recent collection of Ellen Bernstein photographs exhibited in the winter of 2017 at New York's Museum of Modern Art.[5] In terms of dehydration and viscosity, I'd guess it to have been (see Bloch again), somewhere between +3 and +2.8, which is to say it clearly leaned in the direction of the former, but not so much as to be totally encapsulated or to compromise the liquid-solid ambiguity which Alexander Crespin, in the June 2007 issue of *Tricycle, The Buddhist Review*, called "the form-emptiness paradox at the heart of Nasalism."[6] The sensations it produced were almost exactly those which Bloch has called characteristic of an 8 – "insistent but not maddening irritation,"[7] slight pressure against the skin but no "piercing,"[8] "nasal edema," or "respiratory distress"[9] – but in retrospect, there was nothing about it which explains the astonishing effect it was about to have on me.

5   Bernstein, Ellen. *Catalog* (New York: Museum of Modern Art, 2017); *Aperture* July 2017: 24–29.

6   Crespin, Alexander. "The Dharma of Nasalism," *Tricycle, The Buddhist Review* June 2007: 28–32.

7   Bloch, op. cit., 134–135. **Figure 1.**

8   Ibid.

9   Ibid.

❄❄❄❄

Not yet completely awake, Sara yawned, turned on her back, and placed her hands on her chest, the tips of her long slender fingers meeting just below her breasts. If you've read Eldon Partridge's authorized biography of me[10] or, for that matter, the shameless piece by Priscilla Karsh, which had appeared in *Vanity Fair*[11] just six weeks before the morning of which I speak, you know how shaky we were at this point. Like any nine-year couple, we'd known our share of problems, but we'd never been so far apart. We'd met at Harvard, when she was my student during my year as a writer-in-residence, married two years later. In the early days she'd often called us love at first sight, but these days she used the phrase ruefully, if at all, with no small trace (especially in her blogs!) of embarrassment. Everything changed when her career in publishing took off. It didn't help that I'd gotten her the job at Murgate or that she'd been the editor on my last five books, as well as – since I usually wrote so quickly it needed vetting – my blog. For the last three years, in fact, my software had been programmed to email it to her automatically. If she was at her desk, she'd have it edited and back in my mailbox within an hour, and except for those rare occasions when I disagreed with her suggestions, it went back to her when I uploaded it so that, if she liked, she could publish it in the weekly online magazine she edited, *MurgateLive*. We talked as much as always but the listening I'd once been able to count on from her was rarely in evidence. Her nods were halfhearted, her arguments impatient and inflexible, and often as not, her answers began before I'd finished talking. Needless to say, we'd also – as Karsh notes[12] – lost the dependable sex we'd once

---

10 Partridge, Eldon. *Linchak, a Biography* (New York: Murgate, 2011).

11 Karsh, Priscilla. "Linchak at Home," *Vanity Fair* October 2010: 61–65.

12 Ibid.

been able to take for granted. It was rare that we managed it, self-conscious and goal-oriented when we did. In the last seven months, we'd given up trying. It didn't help that she was a star in her office and I close to catatonic in mine. If she'd noticed that I wasn't working, or not at least producing anything but the blog, it was not apparent to me. Her emails, for the most part, were forwards from newspapers, magazines, or manuscripts which crossed her desk, and her IMs were about schedule – parties and openings, dinner invitations, movies, plays, concerts, and readings.

Anyone with the slightest knowledge of Nasalism knows that such alienation alone would have been enough to inhibit my response to the crust with which I had awakened, but even in our early days, when I was free to act on almost any impulse in her presence, her view of the habit we used to call "nose-picking"[13] had never been in doubt. Like most of those whom Marcus Klondyke, in his seminal *Rhinotillexis*, calls "AntiNasalists,"[14] her disgust was clear and unequivocal. The sight of me scratching my nose or even stroking my upper lip could lead her, with a sigh of exasperation, to hand me a tissue. Though she writes in her memoir that I had often "picked" in front of her[15] (indeed, to my amazement and sorrow, she says that my "habit" had once, in our first months together,

---

13 See Natalia Premonova's wonderful history of the word: *Nose-Picking, A Semantic Pilgrimage* (New York: Harcourt Brace, 2011).

14 Klondyke, Marcus. *Rhinotillexis* (New York: W. W. Norton & Company, 2008) 32–56. Various explanations have been advanced for this condition. Klondyke believes the "overwhelming disgust" which characterizes it derives from a dysfunction of the endocrine system, but no one who has studied this habit will be surprised that there are those – Johannes De Kooning, for example, in *The Wisdom of AntiNasalism* (New York: Basic Books, 2008), or Pheobe Hawkinson, in *Healthy Disgust* (Columbus: Ohio State University Press, 2007) – who believe it to be an expression of "maturity" and "mental health." For an excellent, balanced overview of such opinion, see Hamilton Hamm's *Nasalism – Pro and Con* (Moscow: University of Idaho, 2009), and Dean Albarelli's *Nasalism, An Overview*, in *The New York Review of Books*, January 12, 2006.

15 Martinson, Sara. *Then and Now, A Memoir* (New York: Murgate, 2012) 25–26.

made her question her attraction to me[16]), I had always tried to hide it from her, turning my head away, retreating behind a newspaper, sometimes even leaving the room. Certainly, I'd never allowed myself the sort of wholehearted investigation that called to me now.

❈❈❈❈

It's important to note my life was in no better shape than my marriage. I'd never known worse depression. I was drinking too much coffee, watching too much television, spending too much time in newspapers or the Internet. I couldn't remember the last time I'd slept well. Worst of all, after thirty-one years of productivity and, if you'll forgive my immodesty, success as a writer,[17] I'd lost my interest in work altogether. If you've read Harriet Flavor's critical biography[18] or James Fenton's bibliography,[19] you know how prolific I'd been before sinking into this quicksand. From the time I published my first story, when I was sixteen years old, I'd written almost every day for a minimum of seven and sometimes as many as twelve hours. In thirty-one years, I'd published twenty-four books – twelve fiction, ten non-fiction, and two essay collections – as well as an almost uninterrupted stream of articles and reviews which had recently been published – the ninth and tenth of my non-fiction books – in a two-volume set by Murgate. Few were the days when I'd failed to meet the 2,000-word minimum I set for myself, and on good days I could produce 15 or even

---

16   Ibid.

17   Two National Book Awards, a Lannan Lifetime Achievement Award, a Pulitzer Prize, membership in The American Academy of Arts and Letters.

18   Flavor, Harriet. *Walker Linchak, A Critical Biography* (New York: Random House, 2008).

19   Fenton, James. *Walker Linchak, A Bibliography* (New York: Columbia University Press, 2007).

20,000.[20] As Flavor points out, diverse rewards had come to me during the first twenty-four years of my career, but the last seven, when I'd written *The Complete Book of AIDS*,[21] *The Complete Book of 9/11*,[22] and *The Complete Book of Terrorism*,[23] had brought me attention and honor that dwarfed what I'd known before. *The Completes*[24] owed no small debt to the formation – by means of News Corp's merger with Microsoft – of Murgate. Soon after the deal was made, writers in the Murgate stable were given state-of-the-art hardware, sophisticated software, and access to the Murgate mainframe, as well as, of course, fiber-optic access to the Internet and to all the research-training one required. Joining such power to the research staff which Sara had helped me develop and train, I worked more quickly and efficiently than I ever had before. It was a matter of public record that for the last five years I'd received serious consideration for the Nobel Prize. But since the completion of *Terrorism*, I'd produced nothing but the blog. It's true that Norman Harkness, blog reviewer for *New York Magazine*, called it "an account of writer's block which, for candor and anguish, surpasses any we have on record,"[25] but it made no dint in my depression. Like any writer, I'd known my share of gridlock over the years, but my current state was different, all-encompassing. It wasn't just my own work I'd rejected, but language in general.

---

20 In the interest of objectivity, I should note that more than one writer had linked my productivity to hypergraphia, but I have to note as well that I was rarely mentioned alone in this regard. For example, Conrad Negroponski's *Hypergraphia and Other Neuropathologies* (New York: Columbia University Press, 2008), lists 116 writers as "inarguably symptomatic" and many are well known.

21 Linchak, Walker. *The Complete Book of AIDS* (New York: Murgate, 2002).

22 Linchak, Walker. *The Complete Book of 9/11* (New York: Murgate, 2004).

23 Linchak, Walker. *The Complete Book of Terrorism* (New York: Murgate, 2008).

24 Linchak, Walker. *The Completes Boxed Set* (New York: Murgate, 2010).

25 Harkness, Norman. "Blog Update," *New York Magazine* October 2010: 65. See also Clara Adams' review of the edited version of my blogs, published in 2006 by Murgate, in The New York Times Book Review, September 3, 2006.

As I wrote in the blog of June 11, 2010, "More than mute when I sit at my desk, I am disgusted with any thought of writing or reading or the least hint of internal description."[26]

Others may argue (indeed, many have) about the reasons for my block, but even though Jason Friedman had not yet published his celebrated *Culture Glut*,[27] I had no doubt that my problems derived from what he calls the "plague of information which has swept the world since the last decade of the Twentieth century."[28] There wasn't a writer alive who hadn't seen his work trivialized by the flood of information, entertainment, and culture – "the ultimate censorship," writes Friedman[29] – that had engulfed the world like smog. The onslaught of books, film, television, magazines, newspapers, and, most of all perhaps, the endless flood of Internet material had not only swamped the writer's audience with distraction but so diminished its attention span that serious reading had come to seem as anachronistic as typing or traveling by steamship. Books such as Friedman's or Edmund Cleve's *The Word Eclipsed*[30]

---

26   Linchak, Walker. Linchakblog.com, June 17, 2010. Also: *Linchak's Blogs* (New York: Murgate, 2012) 287.

27   Friedman, Jason. *Culture Glut* (New York: Harcourt Brace, 2011).

28   For a painful but accurate account of the situation writers faced even before the turn of the century, see Lawrence Shainberg's "Writers' Prep" in *The New York Times Book Review*, September 11, 1988. Before publication of his novel, *Memories of Amnesia* (Paris Review Editions, 1988), Shainberg attended the first of James Orloff's "addiction clinics" [see David Weller's biography of Orloff, *Anti-Culture Hero* (New York: Harper Collins, 2013), for an extensive description of Orloff's clinics and their international proliferation], which aimed to awaken writers to the fact that an overwhelming number of books, as well as a plethora of entertainment and cultural options, had preceded, would follow, or would appear simultaneous with the one they were about to publish.

29   Friedman, op. cit., 28.

30   Cleve, Edmund. *The Word Eclipsed* (Boston: Little, Brown and Company, 2012) 245. See also *The New Yorker*'s special issue on Information Glut, August 2013; "The Neuropathology of Information Overload," *The New York Times Science Section*, August 23, 2013; and, of course, the definitive study on which *The New Yorker*'s issue was based, *Scientific American*, December 2011. Further and constantly updated information is also available at Glut.com, Informationzero.com, and Braindamage.org, as well as countless blogs which are best found through searching "Information overload" on Google.

would soon explore and quantify the extent and repercussions of this deluge, but obviously, its effects were more extreme for writers like myself. Not so long ago, we'd been able to send our manuscripts to editors and friends with confidence that they'd be received with gratitude and read at once, but nowadays, they were more likely to be greeted with resentment and, often as not, put out with the garbage. How could it be otherwise when every reader's shelves were filled with more than he or she could get to in a lifetime? The truth was undeniable: once a happy love affair, the relationship between writer and reader was now adversarial. It made no difference whether the work was good or bad. Indeed, it's not unlikely that good books, being harder to ignore and requiring more effort and attention, evoked more resentment than bad.

Finally then, my struggle was anything but uncommon. From sociologists like Friedman and websites like Glut.com and Saveusfromwords.com, we had frightening data on the numbers it affected, and from Cleve as well as Peter O'Reilly,[31] we had personal studies of the psychological effects on writers like myself. The former, in fact, quoting extensively from my blog, devotes an entire chapter to the situation in which I found myself.

> "The whole of his adult life had been centered on the act of writing. How was he to live, now that he found it obsolete? What was he to do with his time when, for more than twenty years, seven to twelve of his waking hours had been spent at his desk, producing work which had won him universal acclaim?"[32]

What indeed was I to do? Well, as Cleve so vividly describes, his words almost unbearable for me to read even these eight years later, what I'd mostly done was persist in my routine with

31 O'Reilly, Peter. *War Against Words* (New York: Houghton Mifflin, 2009).

32 Cleve, op. cit., 120–154.

disregard for the pain it caused. If anything, my daily schedule had become less flexible. Every morning I was at my desk by eight. Except for my usual half-hour break for lunch, which I ate in my office, I never left before six in the evening. As before, I avoided all forms of relief and escape, allowing myself no telephone calls, no music, no walks, almost no activity outside my work except the practice for which I was yearning just then.

Figure 2
Marcus Klondyke.

When finally, a few days after my breakthrough, I did my first Internet searches on the practice now known as Nasalism,[33] I found that my case was anything but uncommon among the population in general. As Patterson has shown, however, no one pursued the practice with more vigor and frequency than so-called "creative" people, and none among them more than writers. Given the bias and contempt which surrounded it in those days, it is not surprising that most of us did it surreptitiously, without serious appreciation or any considered idea of its meaning or value. For all intents and purposes, Nasalism as we know it today was virtually non-existent, PreNasalism not only universal but, until Klondyke (**Figure 2**) identified and described it, completely unknown. In effect, our denial itself was denied. We were all of us trapped in what he calls "the deadly nasal tautology."

> "PreNasalism must first be understood as a state of dissociation. When a PreNasalist lifts a finger to his nose, he is, for the most part, unaware of doing so. Indeed, on those rare times when he is unable to deny what he is doing, he experiences such disappointment with himself that, often as not, he vows that he will never indulge again."[34]

---

33 Where I discovered, among other things, surveys such as Dorothy Patterson's and polls done by Murgate's Gallup division, Roper, and others.

34 Klondyke, *Rhinotillexis*, op. cit., 17. **Figure 2.**

✳ ✳ ✳ ✳

If you saw the recent PBS documentary[35] – *History of Nasalism* – much of this will be familiar to you, but if your knowledge of Nasalism comes only from that film, you are sorely misinformed. It's not easy to criticize a film that includes Denis Haggerty's remarkable footage on the Coribundi Indians[36] and their now-famous picking ritual, not to mention Richard Boynton's fiber-optic studies of crust metabolism and trigeminal excitation,[37] but its repeated reference to me as the "Founder"[38] of our practice seems to me a sacrilege. Anyone with the slightest knowledge of Nasalism knows how little I deserve this title. No mention is made of Klondyke or his extraordinary book,

---

35 PBS, Sherman, M.J. Director, *History of Nasalism*, September 5, 2017. Now available on YouTube.com, PBS Home Video, my own website: Walkerlinchak.com, and Rhinotillexis.com.

36 Shown throughout the month of November 2011 on Showtime, currently available on YouTube.com as well as Haggerty's website: Haggerty.com, and of course, the website he helped the Coribundi themselves establish, Coribundi.com.

37 Boynton, Richard, *Crusts in Process*, 2010. First shown on National Geographic Cable channel, August 19, 2008. It should be noted that, for all his scientific, technological, and cinematic brilliance, Boynton has been criticized for what Marlin Gilgooley (reviewing the PBS documentary for *The Annals of Neurorhinology*, in June of 2011 after its theatrical release two months earlier) calls "rhinology so naïve that it sends one back to AntiNasalism."

"Perhaps because his background is in rhinology," writes Gilgooley, "the great drama of Boynton's footage occurs in the frontal sinus. No one could argue with his images of crust origination there or with the succeeding images of crust expansion and descent through the superior turbinate and eventual coagulation in the maxilla, but how is it possible that, at this point in time, educated as we've been by Linchak, Fawck, and Klondyke, work financed by the National Institute of Health should ignore the neurophysiology that catalyzes such rhinology? Is Boynton unaware of Nelson Plaque's recent survey of rhinologists which showed that 78.9% thought it more likely that crust formation is initiated in the enteroventral striatum in the midbrain?"

38 It's true that Sherman is not alone in his misunderstanding. See Janet Hanratty's unauthorized biography of me [*Walker Linchak, Authorized* (New York: Disney, 2010)] and Ornette Max's profile in *Vanity Fair*, ("Linchak Reflects," August 2012: 72–74), and, most shocking of all, Yael Kakutani's unfortunate review of my own *The Complete Book of Nasalism* (New York: Murgate, 2013) in *The New York Review of Books* (December 16, 2013).

which was published more than a year before my first nasal blog appeared; of Robert Fawck, whom so many have called our spiritual conscience; of the brilliant Kenyan rhinologist, Maggie Ettingoff, who in my view has done more than anyone else to translate Klondyke's basic research into accessible language and form.[39] Nowhere within this supposedly faithful history was there reference to Peggy Ann Taylor's then-scandalous music video,[40] which, when it appeared on MTV four months before my breakthrough crust arrived, was – according to Viola Brussel's *Nasalism and Media*[41] – the first time serious Nasalism was seen on television. I, Walker Linchak, the Founder? This romantic naïf who, until the crust with which this narrative begins, remained a prototypical PreNasalist, not just inhibited in my practice but laughing at those who weren't? Ignorant not only of my own motivation and repression but the scientific and philosophical, the psychological, anthropological, even theological discourse the practice had generated for years? You would think from the documentary that the revolution which changed this act from a maligned, forbidden habit to a socially acceptable *practice* began with the appearance of my first blogs rather than in the Victorian Age or well before the birth of Christ. Anyone who doubts the former need only look at the extraordinary archive of nasal material which Sigmund Freud[42] collected (**Figure 3**). For the latter, the work of Jordanian archeologist Ari Akmed, collected in Amman's archeological museum as well as the Murgate Institute in Houston, will not only remove doubt but serve as a thrilling affirmation of archeology in general.[43]

---

39   Ettingoff, Margaret. *Klondyke and his People* (New York: Basic Books, 2008).

40   Taylor, Peggy Ann. MTV, August 15, 2010.

41   Brussel, Viola. *Nasalism and Media* (Los Angeles: UCLA, 2009) 12–24.

42   Freud, Sigmund. *Papers of Sigmund Freud*, Library of Congress (Washington, D.C., 2004) 1246–1298. **Figure 3.**

43   Akmen, Ari. "Nasal Fossils in the Nile Delta," *United Archeology* Vol. 78 (Spring 2013) 217–298.

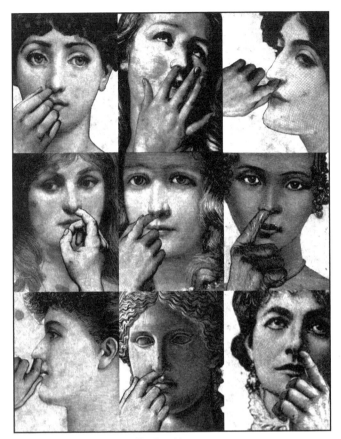

Figure 3 *Victorian engraving from Freud's archives.*

While there are those who think these images fabricated by the researcher – Mary-Claire Gibbons, a confirmed Nasalist who was once a student of Klondyke and is now chairman of the Department of Rhinopsychology at the University of Tennessee – who discovered them in his papers, Freud's admitted passion for nose-picking makes it not at all difficult to imagine him collecting engravings such as this. Many of course credit his Nasalism to his work with German otolaryngologist Wilhelm Fleiss (1858–1928). Fleiss was the originator of a theory called Reflex Nasal Neurosis, which was based on his belief that there was a profound relationship between the nose and the genitals. He treated problems such as "hysteria" and PMS by putting cocaine up his patients' noses and, sometimes, surgically excising an inferior turbinate. Though the Freud-Fleiss letters are well known, Gibbons (quoting an early Fawck blog in which he maintains that since nose-picking and self-consciousness are similarly rooted in subject-object separation, "psychoanalysis is nothing more than sublimated nose-picking") suggests that "AntiNasalists have used Fleiss to deny the significant role that Freud's nose-picking habit played in the development of his thought."

❋❋❋❋

The sun had just begun to filter through the blinds on the eastern window opposite our bed. Bathed in it, spread like a lattice on the pillow, Sara's hair was luminous, darker it seemed than I'd ever known it to be. She was snoring softly, as often when about to wake, or because, as Nathan Meeker suggests in his wonderful review of *The Complete Book of Nasalism*[44] (which begins, as my readers may know, with a brief description of that morning's events) in *The New York Review of Books*,[45] a crust of her own was developing. Much to my surprise, the sound, which usually irritated me, evoked a tenderness which, as often, made me feel that I did not appreciate her enough. Needless to say, however, such emotion did nothing to interrupt the near fanatic concentration I had focused on my nose. I sat erect with determination, my back straight and hard against the headboard. Indeed, without realizing it, I had assumed the posture which neurophysiologist Joanna Lethem[46] has ascribed to the effects of deep-rooted – or what she calls "neuronasal" – crusts on the central nervous system. My spine was straight without being rigid, the small of my back pressed slightly forward, my chin tucked, my head so high that my neck seemed longer and stronger than I had ever known it to be. As Lethem writes, "Every Nasalist knows that certain crusts, at certain moments of one's life, can actually effect fundamental changes in one's relation to one's body."[47] For the first time in my life (but certainly not the last), the equipoise between longing to pick and

---

44 Linchak, *The Complete Book of Nasalism*, op. cit.

45 Meeker, Nathan. *The New York Review of Books*, August 15, 2012.

46 Lethem, Joanna. "The Neurophysiology of Nasalism," *Neurorhinological Perspectives* Vol. 14 (Summer 2007). "Such is the effect of crusts on posture and energy that we have to postulate a direct connection between the nasal membrane and the motor regions of the forebrain."

47 Ibid., 165.

fear of doing so had generated an erection. Lethem, of course, has much to say about this response as well, but if you want to explore the whole spectrum of chemistry and physiology I had just begun to experience, the book to read is Andrea Bench's *Genital Nasalism*.[48]

Sara yawned and stretched and – a sure sign she'd slept well – planted a tender, lingering kiss on my right shoulder. I smelled her hair and felt her cheek on my upper arm. Like many Nasalists at this moment, which Klondyke calls "first awakening,"[49] I noted as if for the first time, almost with alarm, the ambiguous relationship between a deep-rooted crust and the membrane in which it is rooted.[50] One moment it seemed external, tickling and itching, nagging like a spoiled child whose only purpose in life is to monopolize one's attention, the next it seemed internal, beneath the skin, pressing against its surface, increasing in volume and density as if struggling to escape. My erection, of course, persisted. Despite the fact that it seemed to be increasing in size, it was oddly asexual. The whole spectrum of my sensory awareness, after all, was concentrated in my nose. All desire was focused on the crust – to locate and extract it, to be free as soon as possible of the irritation it produced. Bench suggests a commonality between this sort of desire and that which we call sexual,[51] but despite the fact that her CAT and PET scans produce incontrovertible evidence of the motor and neurological connections between nose and genitalia, otolaryngologist Pietro Magnali rejects her views as "superficial"[52] and even "anti-nasal."[53]

---

48   Bench, Andrea. *Genital Nasalism* (New York: Harper Collins, 2011).

49   Klondyke, *Rhinotillexis*, op. cit., 5–27.

50   Bloch calls this "The definitive mark of a neuro-nasal."

51   Bench, op. cit., 217–235.

52   Magnali, Pietro. *The Eros of Nasalism* (New York: Random House, 2014) 176.

53   Ibid.

Extreme vacillation between calm and excitement was my dominant state of mind. The crust, it seemed to me, was vibrating. Intense, almost electrical sensations radiated outward from it – to my cheeks, my forehead, even my ears – and inward, all the way, it seemed, to the center of my head. Most amazing of all, however, was my intellectual condition. My thoughts were not only clear and preternaturally articulate but full-blown visual phenomena, moving through my brain like words on a computer screen. I'd known such moments in my work, of course, but they'd been limited in their production – single words, short phrases, or, at best, uncomplicated sentences. The full paragraph that came to me now was my first indication that the process which had begun with the crust was not just nasal but – as Robert Fawck, more than anyone else, has made us appreciate[54] – neurological. Fortunately my laptop, on the table beside the bed, was as usual booted and open to a blank screen on my word processor. I took it on my lap and typed as if taking dictation:

> "A 'clean nostril' is not just an empty cavity but a non-existent one, a crust which pollutes it so integral and conjoined that there is between them no boundary where one stops and the other begins or, for that matter, no clearly perceived moment in time when this coagulated mass, so recently secreted by the sinus passages, ceased to be part of them."

Anyone familiar with the literature of Nasalism will probably recognize these sentences. Later that day, they appeared on the first of my nasal blogs[55] and two days after that, they became the first paragraph of my first article on this subject, "Nasal Revelation," which appeared four months later in *Psychology*

---

54 Fawck, Robert. *Nasal Neurology* (New York: Murgate, 2010).

55 Linchak, Walker. Linchakblog.com, December 5, 2010.

Today.[56] Finally, two months after the day of which I speak, when I began the preface to *The Complete Book of Nasalism*,[57] they became its opening paragraph. Perhaps too you are familiar with the homage paid to them by Robert Fawck himself, four days later, when he discussed my blog on his own:

> "To read Linchak is to understand that the urgency and even the physical irritations of crusts derive from one's intolerance for their spatial and temporal contradictions. So urgent is the mind's yearning for distinction between 'inside' and 'outside' or, more precisely, 'me' and 'not me,' that such yearning may well serve as the root cause of the habit we used to call nose-picking. It is no exaggeration to say that, since every crust is an active, even aggressive defiance of such distinction, each of our nasal secretions is an opportunity to confront the essential ambiguities of self and identity."[58]

❈ ❈ ❈ ❈

I was just about to close my laptop when an IM from George W. Bush appeared on-screen. If you've read *The Complete Book of Nasalism*, not to mention of course, Ellen Cavanaugh's *Bush and Linchak*,[59] which Sara published just a few months after he left the White House, you know that it was not unusual for us to be in touch. By telephone, email, or, as now, IM, we'd maintained our friendship since we'd shared a room (and I have to admit, at least one girlfriend) in our freshman year at Yale. Over the years, I'd done nine different articles about him, beginning with one for *The New York*

56   Linchak, Walker. "Nasal Revelation," *Psychology Today* April 13, 2011: 52–55.

57   Linchak, *The Complete Book of Nasalism*, op. cit., 1.

58   Fawck, Robert. Rfawck.com, August 15, 2011.

59   Cavanaugh, Ellen. *Bush and Linchak* (New York: Murgate, 2009).

Times Magazine[60] when he was governor of Texas and, most recently, a long clinically detailed *New Yorker* piece (quoted extensively by Oprah Winfrey in the segment she did from the clinic where he was being treated) about the depression which had more or less immobilized him since he'd left the White House. Despite the fact that we were on opposite ends of the political spectrum – I disagreed with few exceptions about his principles and decisions – we'd survived our differences, even come to appreciate each other's distance from the loops in which we worked and traveled. Many of my friends, and more than one critic,[61] had taken me to task for our friendship, calling it proof that my own political views, as a far-left liberal, were either "superficial"[62] or "opportunistic,"[63] but like many who knew him, I'd always found him congenial, even warm, a happy escape from serious conversation. It didn't hurt that, despite his reputation as a non- or even anti-intellectual, he'd been a fan of my work since the early days, when I was writing for *The Yale Review*. Indeed, he'd sent sales of *The Complete Book of 9/11* through the roof when he called it, on "Larry King Live," "the best of the books the disaster generated."[64]

That morning, as often, he wrote to touch base, not for conversation. As he said on "Oprah," loneliness was the worst of the problems he faced in the clinic. He sought connection every chance he got, reaching out, to me and others, almost every day. "What's up?" he wrote.

"Nothing much. You?"

---

60 Linchak, Walker. "Bush Governs," *The New York Times Magazine* April 16, 1998: 54–55.

61 See especially Susan Birra in her review of *The Complete Book of AIDS* (*The New York Review of Books*, August 15, 2002).

62 Edwards, Marvin. *New York Magazine* July 14, 2004: 15.

63 Thomason, Michael. *The Nation* December 19, 2008: 67.

64 CNN, "Larry King Live," December 14, 2004. See also YouTube, of course, and the recently issued collection *Larry King Highlights*, Murgate Media, 2017.

"Fucked up. No improvement. Maybe a little worse."

"Taking your meds?"

"Sure. They don't do shit for me."

"Sorry."

"No need for that. Brought it on myself."

Checking the clock after closing my laptop, I saw that seven minutes had passed since I'd awakened. It was then I realized, for the first time in my life, the depth of the process in which I was engaged. In this short time, as a result of the crust and the concentration it had elicited, my state of mind had completely changed! For the first time in months, I was free of depression!

Don't misunderstand me please: the habit toward which I was drawn at this moment was anything but unknown to me. I knew I'd been doing it all my life, but like any PreNasalist, I'd been oblivious to the gifts it offered. As you know if you've read Klondyke, this is the classical distinction between PreNasalism and Nasalism.

> "Permission to pick, of course, is found in PreNasalists and Nasalists alike. What distinguishes the latter from the former is appreciation and awareness, the mental alertness which undercuts dissociation and makes the practice energizing rather than soporific."[65]

Needless to say, as a longtime PreNasalist, I was not in the minority. According to the first poll taken by Gallup in 2010, the great majority of Americans were PreNasalists at this point in time: 91.9% of respondents called their habit "frequent" and/or "pleasurable" but less than 7% called it "important," and of this group only 4.5% considered it "helpful."[66]

---

65 Klondyke, *Rhinotillexis*, op. cit., 123.

66 Gallup Poll. "Nasalism," August 3, 2010, Gallup.com. Among writers, of course, the percentage in each case was higher. In a study done by Harriet Flavor two years later, (*The New York Times Book Review*, August 2012) 98.5% called themselves "frequent" practitioners, 22% of those professed "mild," and 2.3 "avid" appreciation.

The discovery of the habit's effect on my mind did nothing to diminish my bias toward it. Even as it exhilarated me, I continued to think it impolite and unhygienic, an esthetic nadir, the epitome of distaste, and more than a little neurotic. Shadowed by such contradiction, the situation in which I found myself was not so far from traumatic. Fortunately, I'd already made the essential Nasal turn which, as Fawck and others have noted, increases one's tolerance for trauma itself. My fear and disorientation had almost no effect on my exhilaration. I'd never known a moment so infused with ambivalence or so remarkably at ease with it. Though dismayed by my obsession with the crust, I was no less interested in dismay than I was in my nose. Finally, it seemed a sort of confirmation of its validity that my state of mind struck me as absurd. By this time, my impatience to get at the crust was almost unbearable, but I derived from it the inverse profit Fawck has called the "basic grace of Nasalism":

> "A great crust is a global experience. When attention is totally monopolized by it, it seems to be the only imperfection in one's life. It is no exaggeration to say that when it reaches full maturity, a significant crust embodies, for its host, every imperfection in his life. In the whole of existence, nothing is wrong that its extraction will not correct. One will never know a finer concentration or, in the wake of extraction, a more unqualified contentment."[67]

I know from blog response that many of my readers like to think me liberated at this moment, but nothing could be farther from the truth. Believe me, please: the more I focused on the crust, the more confused I felt. Let's not forget that the object of my concentration not only irritated me but filled me with disgust. Even so, I was on my way. I could not turn back. As I've noted, faith in Nasalism is not simply unaffected but reinforced by the confusion it engenders. So quick was my vacillation

---

67   Fawck, Robert. Rfawck.com, July 12, 2011.

between attraction and revulsion that the distinction between them had almost completely disappeared. An advanced Nasalist will recognize such "dialectical incongruity"[68] as the great gift of our practice, but I was nowhere near such maturity yet. All I knew, at that moment, was uncertainty and groundlessness. Logical thought had always been my ultimate priority. How could I deal with the fact that the thoughts in which I found myself immersed struck me as preposterous?

❇❇❇❇

Changing fast, the crust increased in volume and density and, of course, the discomfort it produced. Needless to say, both the urge to get at it and my annoyance with Sara, whose very presence prevented my doing so, increased in tandem with these sensations. Not for nothing does Helmut Gorky include self-confidence in the famous list of "nasal virtues" which he published recently on Otolaryngology.org.[69] My lack of confidence was every moment demonstrated by the fact that extraction seemed impossible as long as Sara lay beside me. But now a miracle occurred. Just when it seemed I could no longer restrain myself, she got out of bed and went to the bathroom! In all our years together, even these last seven months, she had begun every day by turning to embrace me, but suddenly, without a word or even a glance in my direction, she'd set me free!

Needless to say, my finger rose before she was out of the room. Awe is not too strong a word for the sensation evoked by the reflex. The gesture might well have been activated by a force field, as if between finger and nose there existed an attraction virtually magnetic. "Polarization," neurochemist Janet Greene

---

68 Fawck, Robert. Rfawck.com, October 11, 2012. See also his *Nasal Metaphysics* (New York: Pantheon, 2013) 18.

69 Gorky, Helmut. "Nasalism: Virtues and Deficits," *Otolaryngology.org* (August 16, 2017).

calls it. "Finger and nose act as positive and negative poles, creating what amounts to an electrical current between them."[70] Little wonder that some of the most definitive research into this practice has been done by physicists, like Steven Flanagan[71] or Gary Fishman,[72] who specialize in electromagnetic fields. Only recently has its biology become as clear. The elegant experiments recently reported by Dennis Petersen in *The New England Journal of Medicine* have demonstrated that Nasalism is basically an immunological process, the body rejecting foreign matter as it might a transplanted organ. I doubt that anyone familiar with the research would argue with Petersen when he says that the impulse which caused my finger to move was "essentially an allergy attack."[73]

Though the distance between my lap and my nose cannot have been more than nine or ten inches, a weird trancelike distortion skewed my awareness. The difference between fast and slow was altogether absent from my mind. I had no idea how much time had elapsed between the moment when my finger rose and the moment when it touched my nose.[74] Taking a further leap into the depths of the practice, I had entered that state of conceptual ambiguity which Fawck has called "de-egoing"[75] or,

70   Greene, Janet. *The Physics of Nasalism* (Chicago: University of Illinois Press, 2011) 34–98.

71   Flanagan, Steven. "Nasal Quanta," *American Physics* Vol. 87(June 2010) 219–239.

72   Fishman, Gary. "Electromagetism in the Sinuses," *Scientific American* August 2008: 69–75.

73   Peterson, Dennis. "Allergy and Mucus," *The New England Journal of Medicine* July 2017: 44–53.

74   For interesting work on nose-picking and temporal perception, see "Time and Nasalism," by George Enoulace, in the February 12, 2013 issue of *Rhinology News*. Not to be overlooked however is the data on which Enoulace based his equations, the motor studies of the Texas Tech neuro-orothopedist Harriet Sherman, which measure the speed of "first response" in relation to the volume of crusts and the depth of their attachment to the membrane and, of course, initial trigeminal activation. See Sherman's sublink at Floridauniversity.edu for data which she continues to update regularly.

75   Fawck, Robert. Rfawck.com, August 14, 2011.

in his later work, "deegoing."[76] It wasn't just "fast" and "slow"
I'd lost. It was nose and finger. Was my nose touching my finger
or vice versa? In effect, I was experiencing for the first time
the "identity-bifurcation" which in Fawck's view is not (as some
argue[77]) a matter of perceptual distortion but, as he notes in a
blog I'd come upon two days later, "a liberation from the basic
incarceration of self and personality."

> "Given such basic ontological uncertainty, how can one
> know where to locate oneself in space? Am I my finger,
> my nose, neither, or both? About to pick or about to be
> picked? Finally, am I responsible for this behavior or is it a
> predetermined organic continuum with regard to which my
> conscious decision-making apparatus is irrelevant?

> "Profoundly affecting self-evaluation, the implications of
> these questions are both ethical and neurological. If I don't
> know where to locate myself, whether I am picking, picked,
> neither, or both, how can I be responsible for the act in which
> I am engaged? Finally, who is to say that the embarrassment,
> disgust, and self-reproach one feels at moments like these,
> not to mention the contempt it arouses in others, are not
> themselves neurological responses deriving from the cortical
> brain's rebellion against an act from which it has been
> excluded?"[78]

I heard the toilet flush as my finger, crossing what Fawck's
disciple, Alva Harrison, has called "the last existential
boundary,"[79] made contact with the crust. Needless to say, I
was seized with anxiety. Once again, I had to face the fact that,

---

76 Ibid., December 1, 2012.

77 See especially Friedman, Samuel. "Fawck's Delusion," *Otolaryngology Today* May
2012: 12–15.

78 Fawck, Robert. Rfawck.com, Jaunuary 18, 2012. It should be noted that it was this
blog in particular that annoyed Friedman.

79 Harrison, Alva. "Existential Nasalism," (PhD thesis, New York: New York
University, 2015). Also published on her own blog, Alvaharrisonblog.com, as well as
Fawck's.

for all the changes I had undergone, I was still at the mercy of lifelong habits of etiquette, self-effacement, and repression, not to mention my basic fear of Sara or, for that matter – as my brother Mickey, a psychoanalyst whose views of me are never less than categorical, has always maintained – women in general.[80] But as before, I found myself elated by anxiety. It was almost as if nothing so convinced me I was doing the right thing as the conviction that it was wrong.

Did I say an 8? When finally I made contact, I found myself up against such elusiveness and intransigence that it might have been a 9 or a 10. Attached, as I've said, to the septum as well as the cartilage, entirely devoid – on its outer edge, where my finger connected with it – of the adhesive properties[81] which are the basis for any sort of leverage, it seemed less an insensate cluster of tissue than a cornered insect fighting to escape.

In comparison to the attention I fixed on my nostril now, the concentration I'd known before seemed almost flaccid. How many memoirs, how many poets have celebrated this moment? The crust was no longer an irritant but an adversary. The need I felt to get at it was more like rage than determination. And when, after seven or eight attempts, I mastered it at last, the pleasure I felt was as unqualified and triumphant as any I've ever known.

Not for nothing have so many related the sensation one feels at this moment to those produced by cocaine or alcohol or surfing the Internet. Like all crusts of this magnitude, anything above a 5, for that matter, I felt it separate at multiple points in my nose and sinuses, even my head. It was as if each of its long trailing roots had its own adhesion to overcome. Consider

---

80 Linchak, Mickey. Personal email to me. Elaborated two months later on Micklinchakblog.com, April 16, 2009. "Well I know, being so much like him, that every time he picks, he is inundated with the fear and timidity which has led him, all his life, to ignore his essential needs in favor of the need to please and be loved by women."

81 For an excellent analysis of these adhesive properties, see Martha Elderhorn, "Mucoid Adhesion," *Science* June 2008: 81–85. Also, Elderhorn's compendious website, Elderhorn.com.

this orchestra of union and disunion, this explosion in the central nervous system! Consider its shocks and chills and pulses, its vibrations, illuminations, its tremulous joy and sorrow, and finally, its close to unbearable impermanence – how fast it develops, how quickly it ends, what yearning and sorrow it leaves in its wake. Not for nothing does poet Edgar Hazzard call it "the cosmic twinge."[82] Since nasal tremors are (as Klondyke's student, otolaryngologist Peter Andre, has quantified in his remarkable equations[83]) proportional to the volume and adhesion of the crusts that produce them,[84] it was no surprise that at this moment, awake to the practice for the first time and conquering what may well have been the most elusive crust of my life, I experienced what Fawck has called "the goal to which every Nasalist aspires every time he puts a finger in his nose"[85] – the belief that I had extracted, not just a clot of mucus, but a piece of my own brain.[86]

Emerging naked from the bathroom, Sara went to the

---

82   Hazzard, Edgar. "Fingertip Blues," *The Collected Works of Edgar Hazzard* (New York: Bantam, 2014) 23.

83   Andre, Peter. "Rhinotillexic Equations," (PhD thesis, Missoula: University of Montana, 2007).

84   Surprisingly, Bloch disagrees with Hazzard, maintaining (in her blog) that intransigence and size are for the most part unrelated. "Some 8s and 9s are quickly extracted… but now and then a 4 or a 5 can evade all attempts at leverage."

85   Fawck, Robert. Rfawck.com, June 5, 2009.

86   Lethem, we should note, believes this to be "not at all an apocryphal, not even a lyrical description." But Fawck, while respectful of Lethem, calls this view – in his recently published *NeoNasalism* (New York: Murgate, 2017) – "overly literal." "Ultimate breakthrough crusts," he writes, "produce such transcendence of the material body that there is, for all intents and purposes, no brain from which a piece could be removed." Loathe though I am to argue with Fawck on this or any other subject, I'd be less than responsible if I did not mention Carlita Mengino's recent work on the composition of crust cells, which shows them to be remarkably similar to neurons. Whether this confirms Garcia Malafreda's hypothesis, presented last year at the annual meeting of the American Academy of Rhino-Neurologists, that crust cells are "capable of perception and perhaps even thought," is an issue on which, as I said in my role as a discussant of Malafreda's work at that same meeting and wrote later on my blog, I am unqualified to express an opinion.

window and opened the blinds. Given the degree to which my perceptions were sharpened and intensified, it is no surprise that she'd never looked so beautiful or that the burst of sunlight that filled the room seemed to focus on my fingertip. Offering the crust, which dangled inches from my nose, all the clarity and definition it had lacked just an instant before, it made it seem hyper-real, like a photorealist drawing of a digital image on a computer screen. I felt a sort of awe as I contemplated its various paradoxes. It was linked to me but separate, a clot of foreign matter which my body had secreted and excreted. Once an irritant, it was now a source of tranquility, contentment, and, dare I say, accomplishment, which was not in the least compromised by the familiar waves of revulsion and disgust it was, to my astonishment, evoking once again. Both internal and external, an utter insult, as Fawck so often reminds us, to the part of my mind that sought to comprehend or describe it, it was not just ambiguous but an experience of ambiguity in comparison to which everything I'd called ambiguous in the past seemed distinct and categorical.

Turning to face me, Sara gasped and closed one eye as if unable to believe what she saw. "Do you want a tissue?

TWO

Her face was a mix of anger and disgust which, to my annoyance, had me sexually aroused. Many have commented on such arousal and the negative response that produces it, but I was new to it and perhaps – as we know is not uncommon – more aroused for being so. I held the crust aloft as if to make a point emphatically. I was not unembarrassed, of course, but my discomfort lacked conviction. Many Nasalists know this basic re-arrangement of mind: priorities once absolute, even as they assert themselves, seem dubious and incidental, even cowardly.

"What are you doing?" she said.

I looked away.

"Answer me, Wally."

"What was the question?"

"You heard me. I'd like to know what the fuck you're doing."

My eyes were fixed on the crust. A riveting thing it was, dangling from my finger like the exudation of a wound. Like those which had preceded them, the feelings it engendered – pride and self-doubt, excitement and fear, attraction and revulsion – seemed to contradict each other, but with regard to contradiction, I continued to be equivocal. I wasn't altogether sure I did not find it intoxicating. The crust was striated, rippled, surprisingly varied in color, its peripheries irregular and, it seemed to me, in flux. It was less dense than I'd imagined it to be, more fluid, complex, and, how shall I put it, more subtle. It seemed a miracle that my body had produced it, that only minutes before it had been, as I continued to believe, an integrated and, who knows, even functional part of my brain. Was it possible, as Edgar Varick suggests,[87] that it actually contained neurons or was Mengino correct in her view that the chemistry and anatomy of crust cells was so like that of neurons that distinctions between them is nothing but "anatomical distraction"?[88] Were they still, as Fawck so frequently asserts, communicating with each other? Remember please that, as the author of a book on the mind-brain problem[89] which Norman Mailer once praised in *The New York Review of Books*,[90] I was anything but ignorant about the neurosciences. At that moment, it seemed entirely possible that the object hanging from my finger contained an electrical and/or chemical network of the sort that facilitates information processing. Though its actual composition was, of course, unknown to me, it looked to be as animated as protoplasm under a microscope. Such was my excitement and the looseness of mind it inspired that it seemed less than completely bizarre to think of it as a being with self and mind and ego. This despite the fact that, clearly in flux, changing in shape as well as texture, its ambiguity was so complete that it seemed not only formless but without history or possibility of form. Internal and external, both part and not part of me – how could it be described or comprehended? What does it teach us about what one calls "my body" or even "me," that

---

87   Varick, Edgar. "The Neurochemistry of Mucus," *Scientific American* July 2013: 103–109.

88   Mengino, Carlita. *Scientific American* September 2013: 4. In a letter answering Varick which appeared in the same magazine two months later.

89   Linchak, Walker. *Knowing and Being, Body and Mind* (New York: Murgate, 1989).

90   Mailer, Norman. *The New York Review of Books* February 16, 1990.

newly extracted tissue can seem both part of oneself and alien? The anxiety I felt at this moment was even more extreme than before, all the more so because the sensations attendant to it were not clearly distinct from euphoria.

Sara's eyes were fixed on me. Palpable and aggressive, her disgust, as most of us know who've crossed the bridge that I was crossing at this moment, was not so far from violence. Despite our nine years together, I continued to feel a first-time awareness of her beauty, but then again – perhaps because, as the Czech neurophysiologist Jaroslav Hetsch maintains, "the altered state of consciousness which some call 'Nasalism' is first of all a form of amnesia,"[91] – almost everything I encountered from then on would seem fresh and unfamiliar. Whatever the reason, I can say without a doubt that, for me, at this moment, Sara was almost a stranger to me. In his *People Magazine* profile, Karl Makens describes her as "languid,"[92] but I think this is because he interviewed her on a bad day. Fifteen years of Yoga, running, and diligent vegetarianism had made her supple and robust, and of late, using the gym we'd installed in our loft, she'd added weight training to her workout. She had broad shoulders and small firm breasts and pale green eyes which could, as now, fix with a force that made almost anyone look away. In the early days, I'd found them captivating, but we weren't together more than a year before they began to intimidate me. The feature I liked most in her thin, asymmetrical face was her slightly hooked nose, which she disliked. Paul Edwards, who interviewed her for *Yoga Journal*,[93] did not exaggerate when he called her "traffic-stopping," but it is important to note that his article was written four months after the transformation which, by means

---

91 Hetsch, Jaroslav. *Nasal Neuropathology* (Berkeley: University of California Press, 2012). In fairness, I should note that Hetsch used the "repetitions" of my blogs an example of the "dysfunction" he describes.

92 Makens, Carl. "Sara Martinson," *People Magazine* July 5, 2010: 32.

93 Edwards, Paul. "Sara Martinson," *Yoga Journal* June 2010: 26–27.

of Nasalism, she was about to undergo. Her PreNasal face was equable, almost stoic, but too expressive of her mood. One could read her thoughts on it, watch her confidence come and go. Not that it disappeared often. Insecurity was something she kept to herself or, for that matter, from herself. She had fine, dark, stringy hair which she rarely combed and constantly fingered, and a birth-defect, half a forefinger on her right hand, which would make her practice, once she embraced it, awkward and – for me at least – endearing. The *People Magazine* photograph was less than flattering, but an accurate, almost glamorous one by Ellen Benjamin accompanied Alexi Jamison's profile of her in *The New Yorker* last January.[94]

As always when she was angry, her voice grew deep, almost masculine. I was more than a little unhappy to see that this aroused me as well. On his pseudonymous blog, which he always emailed to me, my brother, Mickey – calling me "W.L." and her "his wife" – had once called her energy "phallic." "It's not awfully far-fetched," he said, "to say that their relationship is homosexual."[95]

"Would you like to tell me," she said, "what's hanging from your finger?"

"You know what it is," I said.

"Yes, it's true, my dear. I certainly do."

"So why do you ask?"

She closed her eyes and made a gagging sound.

Responding to the blog in which I described this event, Mickey (first on his blog and then – fictionalizing me, as usual – on his TV show) accused me of being disingenuous, "pretending to helplessness about behavior which was totally willful,"[96] but as I wrote in that same blog, "Nothing in my life

94 Jamison, Alexi. "Sara Martinson," *The New Yorker* January 6, 2018: 72–75.

95 Linchack, Mickey. Underblog.com, August 16, 2009.

96 Ibid., August 12, 2009.

has astonished me more than the two sentences which had just come out of my mouth." It was not simply that I had been uncharacteristically short with her. My voice was more resonant and even slightly different in accent from the one to which I was accustomed. We know now, of course, that such apostasies are anything but uncommon with Nasalists. This was yet another sign of changes in my neurology,[97] the first appearance of what Partridge calls my "PostNasal self"[98] and, more important, the first sign of the assertive, always-in-flux identity which others, as well as I myself, would often make the mistake of calling "the Founder."[99] Yes, I have to acknowledge it: for the first time in my life I suspected I might be harboring another identity. As a man who'd done two books – one fiction,[100] the other a collection of interviews and profiles[101] which Joyce Carol Oates called "riveting" and "brutal" in *The New York Times Book Review*[102] – on Multiple Personality Syndrome, you can imagine the horror with which I greeted this possibility, but among the numerous points-of-view circulating in my mind,

---

97 See Bench's PET scans again for concrete proof of such effect.

98 Partidge, op. cit., 23.

99 For an interesting, if (to me) painful illustration of this confusion, See Maria Nathanson's bio-pic, *The Founder and I* (YouTube, first appearance, July 16, 2012. Also shown on HBO, the History Channel, and, twice at least, Spike TV.). Despite the fact that Nathanson's subtitle – *Walker Linchak, An Imaginary Portrait* – allowed her to libel me without legal consequences, it did nothing to assuage the trauma I experienced when it was released.

100 Linchak, Walker. *You and Me* (New York: Paris Review Editions, 1982).

101 Linchak, Walker. *Mind Adrift* (New York: Paris Review Editions, 1983).

102 Oates, Joyce Carol. *The New York Times Book Review* April 18, 1982. See also Janet Hirst's discussion of both books in *Psychology Today*, August 1985, a issue devoted to Multiple Personality Syndrome; and the PBS "Nova" documentary on the same subject, which flattered me with attention to the books and an extended, in-depth interview on the same subject which itself evoked considerable response, email as well as snail mail, to the magazine as well as my blog. The latter, broadcast first on August 19, 1986, was released as a DVD by PBS Home Video in 1987. According to Videosales.com, it continues to sell despite the fact that it remains available on PBS.com.

one at least, possibly the Founder's, attributed such anxiety to my old, PreNasal self. Yes, it's true: I was seized with the fear that I'd suddenly become a "Multiple." Dissenting voices continued to have what rhinopsychiatrist, Jason Frederick, in his well-known *Nasalism and Multiple Personality Syndrome*, calls "believable presence in the brain."[103] I heard a female voice cry, "For God's sake, wipe your finger!" and, several times in quick succession, a voice much like my father's: "Get a grip on yourself!" Further complicating things was the fact that I found all such commands credible. Indeed, the fact that I ignored them with a feeling I took to be single-minded seemed nothing if not perverse. Once again, it crossed my mind that nothing improved my mood like indifference to it. It was as if the crust had not just disorganized but rearranged my brain, so that what I'd once taken for its ruling, central voice seemed like weak, transparent posturing. How is it possible that there are those,[104] even among his colleagues, who continue to doubt Fawck's assertion that "Nasalism is essentially a process that re-programs the biocomputer"?[105] The operant feeling was a combination of neither having a choice nor seeking to, of forward motion with complete abandon into realms I could not comprehend.

I heard now the words with which, seven months later, she

---

103   Frederick, Jason. *Nasalism and Multiple Personality Syndrome* (New York: Basic Books, 2009). Though he is generally recognized as the principal authority on this syndrome and its relation to Nasalism, there are many who (on blogs as well as direct email to him and me and Fawck) question whether Frederick, as he claims, originated this specialty or ought more accurately to be known as one of Fawck's most important disciples. For a definitive overview of this controversy, see Carolina Johnson's article on this controversy "Nasalism and Multiples: An Overview," which appeared on Multiplepersonality.com in April 2012 and, as of this writing, remains available there.

104   Edward Akins, for example-n "On Nasalism," *Vanity Fair* June 2013: 47–49; Norma Principal, in *The New York Times Magazine*, August 2013.

105   Fawck, Robert. *The Neurology of Nasalism* (New York: Murgate: 2012) 34.

would begin the memoir that some[106] regard as the finest our movement has produced: "'I'm counting to ten. I swear to God, Walker – if you haven't wiped your finger by then, our marriage is over.'"[107]

As Partridge notes, my background was "classic PreNasal."[108] Though nose-picking ran in our family, as it did in most, the basic attitude toward it was – again, as in most – profane and hypocritical. In my earliest memories of my mother's father, the stern, arthritic, constantly mumbling white-bearded cheapskate of a rabbi who would die at ninety-six on the footsteps of the synagogue in Sfad is always at it behind his evening paper, holding it up in front of his face so no one can see, then wiping his finger on the want ads or the society page or some other section he has no interest in reading. More often than not, I hear him mumbling prayers in Hebrew as he does so. If I read the paper after him, I often come upon the tell-tale smudge like an oversized punctuation mark, but, of course, I never mention it, and for that matter, since it's a question not only of my respect for him but my own ambivalence about the habit, I rarely acknowledge, even to myself, where the smudge originated.

Neither my father nor Mickey was any less dishonest. We had a small carpeted room we called the "den" where the books and the phonograph and the television were kept, and often as not I saw one or both of them at it there, hunched down in the black leather easy chairs that faced each other from opposite sides of the glass coffee table where the art books and magazines were stacked, one hand holding a book or the paper, the other hanging beside the chair while, hoping to dry it out so as to

---

106   Gamby, Peter. "Rhinotillexic Breakthrough: An Overview of the Memoirs" *The Annals of Rhinology* Vol. 410 (July 2013) 57–65. Many have voiced this view, but none so eloquently or with so much conviction and appreciation.

107   Martinson, op. cit., 23.

108   Partridge, op. cit., 21.

discard it surreptitiously, they rolled[109] their latest crust between forefinger and thumb. As for me, the youngest and, sadly, the most inhibited, I waited until I was alone in the bathroom or in bed at night. I don't know if it was because I was ashamed or because (as Partridge suggests[110] but Hellinger[111] argues) the more profound dimensions of the practice had already announced themselves to me, but picking was already linked with solitude in my mind. I rarely did it in public but I couldn't be alone for more than a minute without my finger heading for my nose.

Needless to say, we never spoke, in the house, of the habit we shared. Like all PreNasalists, we bowed to the cultural taboo even as we violated it, and if by chance we observed someone else inserting, our condescension, typically announced by a wink or an elbow-nudge, was quick and unqualified. Within the house, among the four of us, the only one who treated it honestly was my mother. Fanatical about cleanliness (hard to argue with Mickey when, on the first of his blogs that attacked Nasalism – and the first did not hide my identity or hers – he called her "obsessive-compulsive"[112]) but extremely diffident and fearful of both my father and my brother (not me, alas, not me), she found the habit both intolerable and unmentionable and responded by either offering a tissue or, if she found herself in an uncharacteristically assertive state of mind, whispering

---

109   On the issue of "rolling" as well as other methods of handling and disposal, there is, of course, no end of argument and opinion. See Crust.com, Rhinotillexis.com, and Boogerfree.com for the most active view of the controversy, which is also summarized in Jason Alexander's overview in the 2013 report from the Otolaryngology conference in Las Vegas. To my mind, however, no view of this issue equals that of the Coribundi themselves, whose disposal habits are detailed with close to lyrical precision in Haggerty's report on his first visit with them in *Among the Coribundi* (Cambridge: MIT Press, 2002).

110   Partridge, op. cit., 257.

111   Hellinger, Jacob. *Walker Linchak, A Concise Biography* (New York: Norton, 2006).

112   Linchak, Mickey. Micklinchakblog.com, June 5, 2009.

across the room, "Must you?" or, "Honey, please!" How amazing it is to realize now that this prototypical PreNasalist mother, a woman who once admitted in *People Magazine*[113] that she could not hear the word "nose-picking" without feeling nauseous, would become such a pivotal figure in the history of the movement! In a recent issue of *Rhinology Alert*, Danish psychologist David Crimmins devotes an entire monograph to this irony, how much I owed to her fastidiousness, how much my nasal sensitivity was in fact "an instinct for purification" which my mother, cleaning up behind the three of us, inspired in me when I was young.

> "To whom if not to her does he owe his intolerance for impurity? Where if not in her fastidiousness was born the urgency from which his concentration derives, the conviction that life (as he wrote in blog number 46) cannot continue while one's nose remains unclean?"[114]

❉ ❉ ❉ ❉

"One… two," Sara said. "I mean it, Walker."

She stood and faced me with her hands on her hips. Her anger was clear and fierce. I'd always found it frightening and, despite the fact that either I or the Founder said, "Go fuck yourself," I continued to do so now.

"Beg pardon?" she said.

"You heard me."

Responding no doubt to the lack of humidity in the room, my crust was drying, hardening, and, of course, shrinking.[115] Shorn of its liquidity, more articulated and defined and well

---

113   "Mothers of the Stars," *People Magazine* October 13, 2009: 7.

114   Crimmins, David. "Mother Linchak," *Rhinology Alert* June, 2017: 56–59.

115   See Edith Palmer's article ["Mucoid Devolution," *The Annals of Rhinology* Vol. 383 (April, 2011) 134–147] for a precise description of such changes.

on its way to encapsulation,[116] it looked remarkably like one of the huge "mucasoids" exhibited by British artist Penelope Wilde in her recent show at the Mary Boone Gallery in New York.[117] Perhaps it was because I'd never paid so much attention to a crust that I was astounded by the speed and mystery – the drama! – of its transformation. Not for nothing has Fawck called such metamorphosis "a confrontation with mortality"[118] or Klondyke, "accelerated evolution"[119] or Crespin, in the *Tricycle* article I've already mentioned, "ultimate form, ultimate formlessness, ultimate union of the two."[120] Already my crust approached the condition my father and Mickey sought when rolling forefinger and thumb together before dropping one to the floor. Like so many of us, they were absurdly impatient to jettison, but even then they must have known that there was no reason to be so. Who's not aware that, as now was happening on my fingertip, time alone encapsulates? Air equals dehydration and dehydration solidity, and solidity, of course, what rhinologists call de-glutination.[121] Bottom line: my crust required no help. It would any instant fall away on its own. Its

---

116   Ibid. I am particularly grateful to Palmer for her overview of the equations relating the variables – secretion, atmospheric conditions, crust density, and volume, etc. – which determine capsule size as well as the speed of its development.

117   Wilde, Penelope. *Catalog* (Cologne: Zwirner Books, 2017). For a positive review of this show, see: Kimmelman, Michael. *The New York Times* April 18, 2017. For a denunciation: Hesser, Evangeline. *Art Forum* August, 2017.

118   Fawck, Robert. Rfawck.com, August 18, 2009.

119   Klondyke, *Rhinotillexis*, op. cit., 234.

120   Crespin, op. cit., 30.

121   Many have written about this process, of course, but none so precisely as James P. Frilich, who calls it "a vivid example of entropy." "Nowhere will we find a more dramatic display of the disorder and chaos of a system undergoing spontaneous thermodynamic change." What makes Frilich even more impressive, in my view, is that despite the fact that he is an AntiNasalist, he has persisted in his research, finally arriving at what seems to be the definitive de-glutination equation: $AC = !4.5P/C$, where A equals the initial weight of the crust, C its volume, P is change, and C the quantity of heat absorbed. "Understanding De-glutination," *Scientific American* August, 2013: 157–170.

disintegration had begun the instant it left my nose. Look at it now, less than five minutes after extraction: dark as a currant and not much bigger, defined and dense and – yes, Fawck, as usual, gets it right – *mortal*. Needless to say, it had also lost its plasticity and complexity, not to mention its ability to mobilize my concentration. The sight of it was already evoking nostalgia.

Edmund Harkness, whom I guess you'd have to call Mickey's most formidable adversary, is unequivocal in his view that I was, by this time, if not long before, a victim of Multiple Personality Disorder.[122] Rejecting this diagnosis, which he calls "the Multiple Personality Fad," Mickey's view – voiced most recently on "Oprah," when she devoted the whole of her show to the practice – is that, "like all so-called Multiples," I was "basically a hysteric," with a "remarkable capacity for self-hypnosis." "Let us concede," he said, "that the trancelike state which nose-picking evokes encourages the belief that he is a different person. How can one doubt, however, that this says more about his capacity for trance (which, of course, has played no small part in his literary success) than the vectors defining his personality?"[123] I don't blame him or Harkness for such reductivism. Psychologists and psychoanalysts have a fairly incurable need to believe in the continuity of self. The way they see it, we're always connected, no matter how much we grow and change, to where we started. Memory rules our minds and time our memory. How can such minds comprehend that the value of Nasalism lies precisely in its capacity to unify the countless personalities which circulate within us? *Nasalism is not evolution but revolution.* What I experienced on that joyous morning was nothing short of re-birth.

"What did you say?" asked Sara.

---

122   Harkness, Edmund. "Nasalism and Infantilism" *MPD Journal* Vol. 12 (December 2009) 77–89. "All Multiples have an amoral, psychopathic alter driven by infantile fantasies of omnipotence. How better to indulge it than by picking one's nose?"

123   "Oprah," November 11, 2017.

"I believe it was 'Go fuck yourself.'"

"Three."

The need I felt to appease her was one I'd known since our first days together. Even more dangerous however was another need I'd long had – for her to share my states of mind. There was nothing like the feeling that she was unreachable to make me desperate to reach her. "It's amazing," I said, "how cute you are when you're angry."

"Fuck you," she said.

I nodded toward the swelling of the blanket. "Look at my hard-on."

"And fuck your hard-on."

"Look at it."

"You heard me."

My confusion was increasing. Also, my tolerance for it. I patted the bed beside me. "Sit down, Sara."

"Wipe your finger."

"Sit down."

"Wipe your finger."

"Goddamn it, I said sit down!"

She glared at me enraged but then, to my surprise, did as I'd asked. She sat on the edge of the bed for a moment and then stretched out beside me. A moment later, she leaned to the floor for the Sunday paper, which we'd bought the night before on our way home from the movies.

"Put the paper down."

Leafing through the pile, she found the *Book Review* and opened it to the table of contents. "We'll talk," she said, "when you come to your senses."

In addition to being smarter, more decisive, and tougher than me, she was a faster reader. She'd been timed at 800 words a minute while, even after my speed-reading class, I'd never done more than 500. Perhaps this was why there were always more books (seven at the moment) on her night-stand than mine. She wasn't an ounce overweight but she ate no sweets, no butter, and no wheat products, ordered her salad with dressing on the side and went on seven-day fruit fasts twice a year. On evenings when she ate at home, she went to her study after dinner and read or surfed the web all evening. Three years after I got her the job at Murgate, she became an editor. A year later, she accepted the offer of Howard Unterecker, Murgate's CEO, to edit *MurgateLive*, which had been founded just two months after the merger. Finally, a year and a month before this crust arrived, she'd become a vice president. As you know if you read the Makens piece in *People Magazine*, she read or scanned up to 150 manuscripts a week plus two to three hundred readers' reports on submissions to the magazine. Up at five every morning, she worked out for an hour and a half, made her European and Asian calls, arrived at her office by seven and never left before seven-thirty in the evening. She was never without her laptop or, for that matter, her iPhone, which, of course, contained a cell phone, an audio-recorder, a camera, a video-player, a word processor, and a wireless connection to the Internet. Makens says she took more than a hundred calls a day and received twice that many emails, but in my view, he underestimates both. He's certainly right to say she "never missed a serious movie, concert, or play." She had season tickets to the opera, the ballet, and several independent dance companies, and she was passionate about chamber music. She read *The New York Times* every day and, on the Internet, scanned *The Wall Street Journal*, *The Washington Post*, *The Manchester Guardian*, *Le Monde*, and *The Los Angeles Times*. Television, in her view, was basic research. She was up-to-date on cable and network and, of course, she got Neilsen, talk-radio, blog, and chatroom data every day by email. She subscribed to *The New Yorker*, *New York Magazine*, *Vanity Fair*, *Time*, *Newsweek*, *Yoga Journal*, *Tricycle*, and *People Magazine*, and of course, *The New York Review of Books*, *The London Times Literary Supplement*, *Publishers Weekly*, *Kirkus*, and *Variety*. Now and then she took a week off and went alone to a spa in the Berkshires but never without her electronic gear and a stack of manuscripts, on paper, CD, or backup flash drive.

I'm almost certain that, during the following conversation, I did not know what I'd say until the words came out of my mouth.

"Look at me, Sara."

She put down the *Book Review* and picked up *Arts and Leisure*.

"I said look at me."

She found the table of contents and studied it closely. Despite the fact that both this section and the *Book Review* arrived on her computer every Wednesday, she'd always treated their print editions as if they were new to her.

"Don't make me say it again."

She lowered the paper. "Okay. I'm looking."

"My finger. Look at my finger."

"You're kidding."

"This, Sara. Look at this."

"Stop it, Walker."

"Do as I say."

Were those tears on her cheek? Not since our wedding day had I seen her cry.

"Why?" she said.

"Why what?"

"You're ruining everything. Killing us. Why?"

"Tell me what you feel when you look at it."

"Answer me, Wally. Why?"

"Trust me. Look at it and tell me what you feel."

"You know what I feel. Totally disgusted. Sick of you and what's left of your mind."

"Anything more?"

"More? Sure. I wish I'd never met you. I rue the day. Give me a chance, I'll start over again. All I want is to be done with you."

"Can you say why?"

"Wally! Please!"

"What is this feeling you call disgust?"

"Where did you get that voice?"

"Disgust, Sara. Would you call it positive or negative?"

"Who is it you're imitating? Nicholson? Malkovich? Oh wait, I get it. Bogart! Woody Allen's imitation of Bogart!"

"Disgust, Sara! Tell me about it!"

"Fuck you."

"Sara – this is important. I'm serious. What do you mean by 'disgusted'?"

"How should I know?"

"Okay, I'll make a deal with you: if you tell me why, I'll wipe my finger."

Her eyes were frightened. I'd not seen that since our wedding day either. "*Boogers I've Known*," she said, "The new novel by Walker Linchak. *My Mucus and Yours*." And after a pause, "Some feelings can't be explained. We're dealing here with basic social contract. Private and public, separate and distinct. Remember *Civilization and its Discontents*? Locke, Hobbes, Jung – come on, Walker, you're a literate man! Personal hygiene is not conceptual. It's instinct and emotion. Does that answer your question?"

"No, my dear. It doesn't. Not at all."

It's important to reiterate that all of this was virgin territory for me. The destination toward which we were headed remained as unknown to me as (see her memoir again[124]) to her. It's true that the light had gone on within me, but a chorus of inner voices continued to call my illumination madness.

Once again my words surprised me. "Sara! Listen to me! Embrace disgust! Let yourself be a pig for once in your life!"

"Come again?"

"Your toughness, your rigidity, your pathological need for

---

124   Martinson, op. cit., 134.

order and control. Your fear of the slime that exists within you. Come on, Sara! Don't be a slave!"

She touched her ear with the half forefinger on her right hand. "Slime? Within me? Aren't we, just slightly, exaggerating?"

It was the Founder's voice coming out of my mouth. A tad professorial but not, in my view, condescending. Earned authority, I thought. What struck me in particular was its cadence. It was slow and measured, each word carefully enunciated with the slightest beat between. I lifted the crust and offered up a stream of information which, appearing as it did on the first of my nasal blogs,[125] might be familiar to you. I had no idea, of course, where I'd got such ideas or if they were correct.

"Listen," I said. "On average, your nose produces one of these every fifteen to twenty-six minutes. No, don't shake your head. And don't tell me you don't go after them when you're alone." I paused to look at her and then, surprising myself again, continued with what would become the idea Fawck has called my "single greatest contribution to the movement."[126] "And while you're doing so – here's the point, Sara! – you aren't thinking about anything else! You aren't thinking, period! The instant the finger enters the nose, the mind dissolves! You're utterly liberated from the tyranny of thought! Undistracted! No ambition, no anxiety, no self-consciousness! In other words, free, healthy, totally in the present moment! No, don't shake your head! Stop lying to yourself! You're never so sane as when you pick!"

She stared at me astonished. Much though he'd impressed me before, I was awed by what the Founder did now. "Listen to me. I want you to look at this crust for thirty seconds. That's all I ask. Without flinching."

125 Linchak, Walker. Linchakcrust.com, December 5, 2010.

126 Fawck, Robert. Rfawck.com, January 12, 2011.

"You've got to be kidding."

"No, I'm not. I'm just asking you to trust me."

Sighing deeply, she shut her eyes. On the pillow her head moved slowly from side to side as if she were either rejecting my request or searching for a means to deny what was happening. But a moment later, to my amazement, she inhaled deeply and did as I'd asked, fixing her eyes on the crust for nearly a minute.

"Tell me what you feel," I said.

"Like puking," she said. "My stomach's in my mouth."

"Put your finger in your nose."

"What?"

"You heard me."

"You can't be serious!"

"Do as I say."

"I'm sorry, Walker. This is too tacky for words."

"Do it, Sara."

"Walker, please – "

"What's the big deal? You do it when you're alone, don't you?

"Sure, I do. But – "

"Twelve years we've been together. We have sex with no one but each other. We see each other naked and pissing and sitting on the toilet. We take showers together, masturbate together. God knows how many times I've watched you with your vibrator from a chair across the room. And this one act is forbidden?"

And so at last the miracle happened. Very slowly, as if its weight were almost more than she could manage, her left forefinger rose until it came to a halt about a half-inch from her nose where it seemed to be pointing at it or poised in the manner one adopts when trying to frame a thought.

"Go on!" I cried.

Sighing, she allowed half a knuckle to disappear within. Joy surged within me, a feeling of intimacy and connection with her that dwarfed anything I'd known in the past.

"Higher!" I cried. "All the way! Yes! Like that! No, don't withdraw! Keep it there! Okay! Right! Now tell me what you feel!"

"You know what I feel. Embarrassed, ashamed. Badly fucking disgusted, if you want to know."

"Is that all? Tell me the truth!"

"Well, maybe a little hot, I don't know. I mean, it's kind of dirty, isn't it? Can I stop now?"

"Are you wet?"

"Maybe. Well… sure. A little, yes. Let me stop, okay?"

"No, Sara. Not yet."

Nasalism has given me no greater gift than the surge of love I felt for her now. If you've read her memoir,[127] you know that much the same was happening for her. Like so many couples who've long been together, we often forgot our friendship, how much we actually *liked* each other. If it weren't for picking, we might never have remembered.

"What else?" I said.

"What else?"

"Beside wet. What else do you feel?"

She didn't answer. Fixed on mine, her eyes were distant and mystified, but also innocent and childlike and still, very frightened. But all at once they emptied. It was as if she'd vacated them. Beginner that I was, it took me a moment to realize what had happened. Until now, she'd merely obliged me. The act of insertion had been one of compliance. Not entirely superficial perhaps but, unlike the true Nasal impulse, lacking in purpose or intent. Now she'd encountered a crust. Become aware, as I had earlier, of the mystery and complexity of the landscape she was exploring. In other words, she'd *lost herself in the practice*. Not until I read her memoir would I discover that

---

127   Martinson, op. cit., 113.

she was experiencing, just as I had, the belief that she was touching a part of her brain. All I knew at that moment was that I'd ceased to be the object of her attention. There was nothing in her life but the crust.

She got out of bed and hurried to the bathroom. Pausing at the door, she spoke without looking at me. "Ever since I've known you, you've manipulated me like this. Turned me upside down and inside out and hung me out to dry. Fuck you, Wally. Fuck you. When will you understand? When will you let me go?"

She went inside and slammed the door behind her. A moment later, I heard her vomiting.

I t's a naïve writer who isn't suspicious of euphoria. The disappointment and sadness it almost always leaves in its wake teaches us to regard it with skepticism that can finally become a sort of pride. Certainly, it had become so for me. I took it as evidence of professionalism that the joy I felt as I walked to my office that morning was so interlaced with feelings of apprehension and mistrust that I yearned for detachment more and more with every step I took.

My skepticism was quickly confirmed when I sat down at my desk. Hardly a minute passed before I hit the wall that writing had become for me. Here again was the compulsion to write and the impotence it produced. The muteness. The feeling that my brain had turned against me. Of course I still remembered the calm and concentration my crust had engendered a few hours before, but if anything, the memory embarrassed me. I was seriously afraid for myself. To the voices which accused me of taking leave of my senses, I had no answer at all.

As usual, however, my first response to stress was what Klondyke calls "digital dissociation."[128] The movement of my finger was spontaneous and, at least until it entered my nose, unconscious. *PreNasal.* Had it not been for the awareness to which I had come that morning, I might now have enjoyed

---

128   Klondyke, *Rhinotillexis*, op. cit.

the benefits of what comedian Joanna Mack, in her wonderful sketch on "Saturday Night Live," called "fingertip Prozac" – twenty or thirty seconds of freedom from self-consciousness, a quick deflection of anxiety from the abstract goal of writing to the concrete goal of extraction or, in this case, since no crust called at that moment, the entertainment one derives from the quest itself and its attendant hope, possibility, and suspense. That I had out-grown such "PreNasal superficiality"[129] I discovered now, I have to admit, with a kind of alarm. It was painfully clear that the easy escape of unconscious picking was no longer available to me, and I was anything but happy to realize it. For this, as for so many other obstacles we encounter, we have Klondyke to thank for explanation:

> "The leap from PreNasalism to Nasalism is never entirely free of anxiety and regret. Even those who relish such growth will often feel a kind of disappointment and apprehension as they cease to combine picking with dissociation. One is, after all, closing off an avenue of escape, exchanging unconsciousness for alertness. Once we could count on this habit to put us to sleep. Why be pleased when it wakes us up?"[130]

But if such awareness were reversible, Nasalism as we know it today might not exist at all. Anyone who's embarked on this Path knows that, once one takes the step I'd taken, it cannot be denied. Sitting at my desk just then, I had an illumination even greater than that morning's. Alarmed though I was (and still, believe it or not, embarrassed! Still ashamed![131]) to find my

---

129 Klondyke, *Rhinotillexis*, op. cit., 123.

130 Ibid.

131 See Mary Ann Margolin on "the neurochemistry of nose-picking vanity." Mamargolin@Texastech/rhinology.edu; Nathan Piagre's "Nasalism and Shame," Rhinotillexis.com; also, number seven of my blogs, and Claude Woodman's poem, "Watch Me Pick," first published in *The New Yorker* July 8, 2009: 47, and again in *The Collected Poems of Claude Woodman* (New York: Farrar, Straus, 2011).

finger in my nose, I was suddenly aware that, once again, my state of mind had changed. The need to write had disappeared entirely! I had no need to describe the situation in which I found myself, no need for words at all. Except for the extraction I was seeking to achieve, I was without desire of any sort!

I should note that, about nose-picking itself, my feelings continued to be negative.[132] Not by any stretch could I pretend that I considered it reasonable or acceptable behavior. Waves of disgust coursed through me, but my response to them was unfamiliar. If anything, they exhilarated me. Though I knew nothing of Fawck at that time, of course, I was already experiencing the "freedom from logic" he calls "the first and most dramatic benefit of mature insertion."[133] Not from drugs and certainly not from alcohol had I experienced such conflation of lucidity and irrationality. Confusion no longer disturbed me. The continuing, maddening disorder of my thoughts seemed to me auspicious. As Fawck writes, "From the moment you pick with awareness, you enter a realm in which meaning and logic are obsolete. The slightest moderation of absurdity is sure to exacerbate it."[134]

Adding to my exhilaration was the knowledge that the act in which I was engaged was commonplace. That in all probability there was no one on earth who'd not experienced what I was experiencing just then. It required neither talent nor intelligence, no thrust of will, no surge of inspiration. All one had to do was ignore etiquette and reason, refuse, as I was doing just then, the tyranny of disgust. Thus did I realize for the first time, but certainly not the last, the global implications of the vision I'd

---

132   Fawck, Robert. Rfawck.com, February 10, 2009. In a blog written in July of 2006, Fawck has a wonderful piece on this distaste and the way in which it is often intensified at moments of such epiphany. "There is nothing like nasal epiphany to reveal and/or exacerbate the basic symptoms of hippocampal brain damage."

133   Ibid.

134   Ibid.

embraced. What I was dealing with went far beyond my own personal satisfaction and relief. Anyone alive could know the happiness and freedom I felt now. Is it any wonder Ettingoff calls Nasalism "a path direct as any to unselfishness and altruism?"[135]

Needless to say, my mind was cleared by these connections. The blog was done in half an hour. I held nothing back. If you've read it, you know that what I offered here was my first description of the crust, the irritation and concentration it produced, the desperation to extract, and the joy of doing so. Here was Sara resisting at first, then surrendering, finally rushing to the bathroom, throwing up, refusing to come out until I was gone. Like the paragraph I'd written earlier, as I lay beside her in bed, all of it came in a rush, without inhibition, as if dictated by a mind outside my own.

This first blog contained not only my first description of Nasalism but its initial effect on my work. For all his anti-nasal bias, John Updike did not exaggerate when, reviewing my blog collection for *The New Yorker*, he wrote that "the practice Linchak describes is embodied in his language. Completely driven by the irrationality which those who embrace this habit celebrate, his essays are not just [italics his] *about* Nasalism. They physically embody the practice they describe."[136]

Though positive rather than negative, my own response was not so far from Updike's. As I wrote the following day, in the second of my blogs which were devoted to Nasalism,[137] the deepest truth of this, my first writing about the practice, lay in the discomfort I felt re-reading it. If ever I'd written anything less literary, less disciplined or elegant, I did not remember it. Like my thought-process in general, the blog seemed indifferent

---

135 Ettingoff, *Klondyke and his People*, op. cit., 239.

136 Updike, John. "Books in Review," *The New Yorker* August 19, 2012: 31–34.

137 Linchak, Walker. Linchakblog.com, December 6, 2010.

to reason and logic, not to mention literary craft. How could I ask for greater confirmation of the direction I'd taken?

As I've noted, I'd programmed my software to email my blogs to Sara. Indeed, I often delayed uploading it until I'd heard her criticism. This time, however, I felt so certain of what I'd written that I put it online at once. Instinct told me that, for all her anger and revulsion, her mind was not completely closed to me or to the practice. I could not forget the expression on her face when she'd first contacted her crust. Her vacant eyes were no less an affirmation of Nasalism than the blog itself.

As we know from her memoir, however, my instinct had misled me.[138] When I arrived at home she met me at the door, but the eyes that met mine were no more open than they'd been that morning. "I'm sorry, Wally. You'll have to count me out. I can't go there with you. Call me uptight, middle-class, I won't argue with you. But I can't ignore nausea. I can't ignore throwing up. I have to trust my body."

"I trust my body too."

"I'm not saying you don't."

"And I trust yours."

"But it is mine, isn't it?"

Her face was an amazing mix of fear and anger, agitation and determination. I don't know why, but it gave me hope. "I'm not surprised you vomited," I said. "I took you to the root of your fear."

"Please don't start with that voice again. I can't stand how it turns me on."

"Well, that's your body talking too, isn't it?"

"Not necessarily. I always had a weakness for your mind. But that's my head talking, not my body. Right now, I'd say my body hates your mind."

"Why?"

---

138 Martinson, op. cit., 123–156.

"Because it's capricious and perverse, not to mention disgusting."

"Did you read the blog?"

"Of course I did."

"Well?"

"It reads like J.T. LeRoy or some other phony. Hoax or bullshit, who knows which. No doubt you'll find your readers. You always do. How long's it been since truth had anything to do with what we see on the page? Who knows it better than people like me? But this is life, Wally, not writing or, God knows, publishing. Like I said, I can't go there with you."

"Do you want us to split?"

"Split? Sure I do, but I don't know if I've got the courage."

"Well, whatever you do, I'll support you."

She shrugged and turned her back to me. "There's the voice again."

"Sorry," I said. "It's the only one I have."

"Leave me alone," she said.

FOUR

Though I reviewed it negatively for the *Times*,[139] I have to admit that Jonathan Leiter's *Nasalism and Manic Depression*[140] is not completely foreign to my experience.[141] I can't believe there are many who've embraced the practice I discovered that Sunday morning who haven't experienced the crash I endured on Monday. Check out my blogs. Volatility is a constant, especially in the early days. With each crust producing more discomfort and concentration, each extraction more insight and relief, it's almost impossible to avoid over-the-top excitement.

But I was more extreme, by a lot, than your average Nasalist. With my beginner's excitement combining with the breakthrough in my work, it's not surprising that I woke up euphoric. Any Nasalist would know that I was headed for a fall and it came with my first crust Monday morning. The reversal

---

139   Linchak, Walker. *The New York Times Book Review* April 3, 2012.

140   Leiter, Jonathan. *Nasalism and Manic Depression* (Gary, Indiana: Notre Dame Press, 2012).

141   I'd be sadly remiss not to mention Paul Holloway's answer to Leiter, *Goodbye Depression* (Chapel Hill, North Carolina: Duke University Press, 2012). It is Holloway's contention that "nothing cures Manic Depression more quickly than wholehearted embrace of nose-picking."

was cruel and frightening. It was unremarkable in size, a 4^{142} at most, its extraction quick and effortless, its twinge localized and superficial. No sooner was it extracted, however, than I was overcome with anxiety and depression. Far from the peace I usually felt at this moment, I felt bereft and purposeless, as if completion of the act had left my life devoid of meaning. Ettingoff, as I'd see soon enough when I discovered her website, calls this PED[143] or "Post Extraction Despair,"[144] and Klondyke, devoting an entire chapter to it in *Rhinotillexis Updated*,[145] "our Second Gate." Deprived of picking, one feels deprived of life itself. Worst of all, one is suddenly aware that the habit one loves is dependent upon the capricious whims of the body.

In the early blogs that followed this first encounter with Post Extraction Despair, I did not mention what was most distressing about it. The First Gate cures depression, but at the Second, we meet the fear that the cure is worse than the disease. Such fear hit me very hard. Was excitement about picking just another sign of the degree to which my mind had weakened or abandoned me? Had I passed the point where I could trust my judgment and perception? How could I dismiss the possibility that has especially to be feared by those who've been writing as long as I have, that my so-called "revelation" had been predicated less by real experience than the *yearning to work at any cost*[146] which,

---

142 We should note that Bloch has always been careful to include among her classification scale the possibility of what she calls "idiosyncratic crusts," which defy labels. Indeed, she mentions 4s as particularly likely to "produce effects distinctly at odds with their density and volume…" **Appendix A.**

143 See PED.com as well as Nicholas Coleman's wonderful blog, Nxcoleman211.com and the Wikipedia entries on Nasalism, rhinotillexis, myself, and Klondyke, as well as, of course, PED itself.

144 Ettingoff.com.

145 Marcus Klondyke, *Rhinotillexis Updated* (New York: Murgate, 2010).

146 Countless books, websites, and blogs, of course, address this trap. See especially Hypergraphia.com, Wordpuke.com, Nelson Mangowitz's blog on the subject, which has appeared almost daily since 1999, and of course, the best known book on the subject, *Midnight Disease*, by Alice Flaherty (Boston, New York: Mariner Books, 2004).

of all the needs that drive a writer, is surely the most dangerous and counterproductive. All writers know this need. It kills your inspiration. Writing is breathing and you'll suffocate without it. Had I been poisoned by this compulsion? The need to escape the dreaded muteness at my desk, to believe in language again, to trust the instincts of my mind – had it driven me to the blog I'd written yesterday? Had I embraced nose-picking so as once again to believe myself productive? Worse still, had I chosen this subject simply because my need to be original trumped all other considerations? It was almost as if I were anticipating Harriet Veevers, who'd accuse me, in her review of my blog anthology[147] in *The New York Review of Books*, of "embracing this taboo for its shock value alone."[148]

Please believe me: even in my despair, I did not align myself with those, like Eddington Bruno, who consider Nasalism a form of masochism.[149] I did however recognize, as soon as I felt a little better, what Viktor Petersen called, in a blog which Sara would forward a few weeks later, "the fatal tautology" on which nose-picking is based: "*an act of purification is inseparable from the impurity in which it originates.*" I don't know that I understood the four-part equation which Petersen presents in his famous monograph, but it was surely confirmed by the impossible trap in which I found myself at that moment:

"(1) If an act of purification becomes compelling, its original, motivating impurity must be equally so;

(2) once compelling, an impurity becomes pleasurable;

(3) once pleasurable, impurity will not arouse the yearning for its termination and relief which made it compelling in the first place;

(4) finally: there is no surer way to purify an impurity than to embrace it wholeheartedly."[150]

147   Linchak, Walker. *Linchak's Blogs*, op. cit.

148   Veevers, Harriet. *The New York Review of Books* April 3, 2012.

149   Bruno, Eddington. "Nasal Masochism," *Rhinology Archive* Vol. 213 (August 2012) 29–34.

150   Peterson, Viktor. Vpeterson234.com, January 26, 2011.

In sum: why, if a crust is pleasing, should anyone wish to extract it? How can one take pleasure in sensation one longs to escape?

Even when, a moment later, my anxiety dissolved, I found it difficult to comprehend the fact that relief from irritation, which is, after all, the crux of Nasalism, had left me empty and apprehensive. The problem, of course, was the other side of the equation, that the *quest* for such relief is itself a source of pleasure. There was no gainsaying the illogic in which I was trapped. The inevitable conclusion of the Path on which I'd set out was *desire for the undesirable*. How could I, in the wake of such understanding, pursue my next crust with anything like the determination it required? I think the great British philosopher, Joseph Eggleston, who coined the term "nasal absurdity" in his book of that title, was the first to explore what he called "the wisdom of our contradictions":

> "In view of the fact that the absurdity of the human condition makes 'sanity' and 'well being' synonymous with one's capacity to embrace absurdity, one cannot be surprised that an absurdity like nose-picking should prove to be universally therapeutic."[151]

But then of course one has to face the larger questions which Alexander Harkavy raised in his *New Yorker* profile of Eggleston: "Can absurdity survive appreciation of itself?"[152] Consciously pursued, does absurdity remain absurd? If ceasing to be absurd, does it cease to be desirable? That's the root problem of course. You can't talk about Nasalism without talking about desire. If you've read Fawck, you know that he frequently returns to this theme in his later work. Unlike Eggleston, however, he views the problem neurologically.

---

151   Eggleston, Joseph. *Nasal Absurdity* (London: Oxford University Press, 2010) 67.

152   Harkavy, Alexander. "Joseph Eggleston," *The New Yorker* May 19, 2012: 95–99.

"From spiritual practices as well as the neurosciences, we've long known that desire is the intractable pathology of all human brains. Since it can't be eradicated, its most effective antidotes are rooted in inversion. Desire is nullified when directed toward goals which are irrational or absurd. Consider pinball machines, games like solitaire, newspapers, television. How can we be surprised that Nasalism, fulfilling such qualifications perfectly, is neurologically corrective?"[153]

Though hardly conscious of it, this brief glimpse of PED took me very close to the conclusion advanced by so many AntiNasalists, that the practice is not simply disgusting and masochistic but – as Harkavy put it, a year after his Eggleston review, when Terry Gross interviewed him about his new book[154] – "impossible."[155] You could say that the confusion I faced at that moment was a measure of my nearness to Harkavy and my distance from Fawck. I knew nothing but the contradictions I faced and the bizarre sensation, once again, of being intoxicated by them. The thing about the gates of Nasalism, you see, is that passage through them is rarely uninterrupted. They open easily but they point toward the unknown and away from certainty. The gap is filled with separation anxiety as well as a sense of terrific adventure. Did I realize that, as Fawck once wrote, "we cannot close the Second Gate behind us until its confusion becomes exhilarating"?[156] I can't say I felt exhilarated yet, but the confusion was undeniable. In fact, my state of mind was suddenly so expansive that I reached for my laptop and – writing once again as if taking dictation – began the second of my nasal blogs.

---

153   Fawck, Robert. *PostNasal and Beyond* (New York: Murgate, 2013) 132.

154   NPR, "Fresh Air," August 9, 2012.

155   Harkavy, Alexander. *Tragedy and Taboo* (New York: Simon and Schuster, 2012) 12–24.

156   Fawck, Robert. Rfawck.com, September 5, 2009.

"It is only because crusts strike us as absurd that they annoy us and only because they annoy us that we wish to be rid of them and only because we wish to be rid of them that we're so happy when they arrive. Here is our root exhilaration: Nasalism and absurdity are one! No human activity confronts the rational mind with more defiance and contempt, and none therefore is quicker to alleviate its tyranny. Nasalism without absurdity is like pasta without sauce."[157]

Unfortunately, I was unable to finish the blog just then. As I was – with no little disbelief – re-reading the above sentences, three IMs flashed on my screen. I ignored the first two – from my secretary, Carlotta Torres, and my brother, Mickey – but Sara's was another story. I'd never been able to postpone hers.

"Busy?"

"Little," I typed. "Why?"

"Amazing thing. Gotta talk. Call, okay?"

I clicked onto my video phone and pressed her speed-button on my keyboard. So long I'd called her like this – on the computer, my cell, or the one in my office – that I didn't know her numbers anymore. A moment later her face appeared on-screen.

"What's up?"

"I don't believe it. You won't either."

"Tell me."

Her voice dropped to a whisper. "Can you hear me?"

"Yes."

"In the limo this morning, heading for the office, I imagined you picking and I came. *Boom*. On 6th Avenue and 18th Street."

I have to admit that I wasn't totally surprised. The erotic effects of the practice – everything that Bench and Carelli[158] and, best of all, Sara herself[159] describe – had been clear before

---

157   Linchak, Walker. Wlinchak.com, December 6, 2010.

158   Carelli, Luisa. *Sexual Nasalism* (Cambridge: Harvard, 2008).

159   Martinson, op. cit., 213–246. See also her appearance on "Oprah," June 5, 2013.

she'd rushed to the bathroom. Why else, for that matter, had she freaked out? "Of course," I said. "Why not?"

"'Of course'? Did you say, 'of course'?"

"I guess I did."

"Have you forgotten the woman you married?"

"No. But she's a different woman now, isn't she?"

"Hang on," she said. "This is my Tokyo call."

I watched her talk for a moment and then, shifting her to a smaller window in the bottom corner of my screen, went online. I scanned the headlines, then the stock ticker, sports news and weather, and then, a longtime addiction, switched to solitaire. Needless to say, the anti-nasal establishment, especially Paula Collins, the most vindictive of our critics, has much to say about the similarities of Nasalism and solitaire, especially in its digital form.[160] According to Jason Cundra's recent overview of AntiNasalism in *Shambhala Sun*,[161] Collins refuses to call the practice anything but "nose-picking" or, despite the fact that she equates it with "game-playing," to grant that it is anything other than "addictive" or "pathological."

Three or four games later (I always lose count), Sara (glancing at me and shaking her head with impatience) was still on the phone, so I succumbed to another addiction, Googling myself. I don't remember the actual number of hits, but it was well into six figures. Despite my breakthrough and the freedom from vanity and egoism one is supposed to find in Nasalism, I have to admit I found the display no less exhilarating than before. First on the list, of course, was my own website and blog. Then came the Partridge book, Cavanaugh's *Bush and Linchak*, and a succession of hits on my relationship with Bush. On the right side of the screen, ads listed all the forms (soft-cover and hard, print-on-demand, audio, electronic

---

160 Collins, Paula. *Addictive Nasalism* (New York: Norton, 2012).

161 Cundra, Jason. "Nasalism, Pro and Con," *Shambhala Sun* June 2, 2017: 40–46.

downloads, CD-ROMs, etc.) in which my books were available, plus sites where they could be ordered. I followed the trail to a site that compared my sales to those of other writers and my sales this year to previous years. Another site offered one or another actor reading – on video – from one or another of my texts, and finally, Allbookreview.com provided an exhaustive list of my reviews over the years. I was reading a review of my third novel from *The London Times Literary Supplement* when she returned.

"Sorry. Where were we?"

"You were coming," I said.

"Oh my God, right. Can you believe it?"

"Was it good?"

"Volcanic."

"Single or multiple?"

"Just one, but long. *Really long.*"

"Did you touch yourself?"

"No. I didn't have to! I was reading the paper."

"Do it now."

"Stop it."

"I'm serious."

"No."

"Do it, Sara."

Her hand slid off the desk and disappeared into her lap. Even on-screen, I could see her eyes change.

"Watch me now," I said, doing the same.

"Stop it," she said. "Please. I've got work to do."

"Come home."

"What?"

"I want you. Now."

Her hand reappeared. "Don't be mean. You know I can't. I've got manuscripts on my desk, emails to answer, phone calls, two meetings, Yoga at noon. By the way, have you Googled it yet?"

"What?"

"Picking."

"Do it now."

"What?"

"Put your finger in your nose."

"Tonight, okay?"

"Now."

"Don't press your luck, okay? The Google. Have you done it yet?"

"I was just about to."

"Try it. You won't be disappointed."

As soon as we said goodbye, I followed her advice. You may be familiar with this search. Since my software was programmed to record my surfing, and this one, for obvious reasons, was historically significant, I include it as Appendix A in *The Complete Book of Nasalism*. It is also available, and carefully dissected, in Catherine Hawke's *Online Nasalism*,[162] which is the best, in my view, of all the books that examine the ways in which the Internet and electronic communication influenced the proliferation of the practice.

I'd never done a search that surprised me so much. Any thought that the habit was rare and eccentric disappeared with the first screen. The 221,485 hits included websites, newsgroups, chat rooms, online journals and blogs, more than five hundred (YouTube, Google, MySpace, etc.) videos, commercial sites and of course, on the right side of the screen, the usual scroll of advertising – facial tissue, inhalers, instructional CDs, support groups, and, most important, the drug called "Rhinobate" which, though unknown to me at this time, would soon become as invaluable to me as it was for other practitioners.

The hits were pro and con, personal and professional, scientific, anthropological, and psychological. On the negative side were those who pathologized the habit, relating it to

---

162   Hawke, Catherine. *Online Nasalism* (New York: Murgate, 2013).

Obsessive-Compulsive Disorder, addiction, or other forms of psychopathology. On the positive were renegades, like J.J. Lundy and his Booger.com, which celebrated disgust and its assault on middle-class taste and, within a couple of days, would list my blog along with others which were to be attacked because, as one of Lundy's blogs put it, "they aim to make us respectable."[163] Finally, there were those for whom Nasalism, if not respectable, was worthy of investigation. Among the latter I encountered, for the first time, Patricia Kelman,[164] the Stamford sociologist whose survey is still updated annually. I learned that Peggy Ann Taylor's video was available on YouTube, Denis Haggerty's website offered video of the Coribundi picking ritual, and Fawck's recent essay – "The Ontology of Nose-Picking" – was available on his blog.[165] Here too was James Edgar Geigy's twelve-step program for "addicted nose-pickers"[166] and, also on YouTube, as well as other sites, at least fifteen video blogs, or vlogs, which offered video-streams of picking itself – with close-ups of faces and fingers, of course – as well as, in two cases, close-ups of extracted crusts. On a site called Nasalblog.com, I was pleased to find the one I'd written the day before listed in fourth position. Searching further, I clicked on the *Encyclopedia Britannica*. Its first reference for nose-picking took me to Wikipedia, where I discovered the medical term which, more than anything I came upon that day, showed me how much

---

163 Lundy, J.J. Pickfree.com, August 12, 2009.

164 Kelman, Patricia. Patricia_Kelman@Stanford.Rhinology.edu.

165 Fawck, Robert. "The Ontology of Nose-Picking," Rfawck.com, September 23, 2009 and recently in his collected essays, *Robert Fawck Essays* (New York: Murgate, 2017).

166 Geigy, James Edgar. Though Geigy maintained a low profile at that time, publicizing his workshops strictly on the Internet, he'd soon be persuaded (by the spate of books about him which he called "specious every one of them" on his Charlie Rose interview) to publish his program. See *Pickers Anonymous* (New York: Putnam, 2013).

Figure 4 *Photograph by Ellen Bernstein, exhibited here at Mary Boone Gallery.*

Jeffrey McClendon, writing in *Art Forum* (November 2012) said of this show that "it puts to rest, once and for all, the idea that art and religion are separate tracks in the human mind."

I'd underestimated the habit: "rhinotillexis."[167] Returning to Google, I entered it as my search-word. Among the 11,953 hits[168] which came in response, I found Klondyke's book of that title,[169] Wikipedia entries for him and the book itself, and finally, Klondyke's website, Rhinotillexis.com, and its

---

167 Wikipedia.com. "The act of extracting foreign bodies from the nose with a finger or other object. This is an extremely common habit, with some surveys indicating that it is almost universal, with people picking their nose an average of about four times a day. The mucus membranes constantly produce wet mucus that is exposed to the air. Once dried, the mucus typically causes a sensation of irritation that leads to the compulsion to dislodge the itch via rhinotillexis. However, extreme nose-picking resulting in severe nasal trauma is termed rhinotillexomania…"

168 See Appendix A of Fredrick Nagle's *Nasalism and the Internet* (Milwaukee, Wisconsin: Technobooks, 2013) and Technobooks.org for a complete reproduction of this search result.

169 Klondyke, *Rhinotillexis*, op. cit.

exhaustive bibliography.[170] Searching its sub-links, I found links to Ellen Bernstein and her website, where I was introduced to the first of the crust photographs (**Figure 4**) which would later be published by *Aperture*;[171] Lucille Bloch, whose site described her classification work, which, as I've noted, was then in its early stages (**Appendix A**);[172] Haggerty again; and, finally, Ettingoff's *Klondyke and his People*,[173] which meant more to me than anything else I'd come upon because it directly addressed the problem of Post Extraction Despair.

I doubt there are many Nasalists who aren't familiar with Ettingoff's book. It is the classic text on the Second Gate. Titled *Klondyke and his People*, it includes interviews which she conducted with thirty-one of the forty-seven subjects[174] who participated in the original research for *Rhinotillexis*. For me, this was a godsend: intimate first-person accounts of the leap from PreNasalism to Nasalism or, more precisely, the "permission to pick" which, as Ettingoff says, "launches the practice." Not surprisingly, many of Klondyke's subjects reported vacillations

---

170   At that point in time, this bibliography included 1,265 books, 23,457 articles, 11,235 websites, and 1,268 blogs. Needless to say, these numbers have increased considerably. According to Harriet Simmons' *The Literature of Nasalism* (Oxford: University of Mississippi Press, 2014), the bibliography as of June 2013 included 13,437 books, 132,679 articles, 115,325 websites, and 897,235 blogs.

171   Bernstein, Ellen. *Aperture*, op. cit. **Figure 4.**

172   Crustclassification.com, op. cit. Needless to say, Bloch's website was also listed. At that time, it was actively soliciting photographs as well as other information on crusts. It should be noted that, while admirably resisting temptation to publish her preliminary research, Bloch's website was even then presenting the first of her somewhat crude attempts at cataloging crusts. Needless to say this first image, which continues to circulate on the Internet, has since appeared in divergent formats, including Aldous Prezl's *Nasal Adhesion* (Boise, Idaho: University of Idaho Press, 2000), see footnote #183; Carlos Rodriguez's "Mucoid Adhesion and OCD," *The Annals of Rhinology* Vol. 21 (August, 2000) see footnte #187; as well as, of course, the cover of Bloch's last book, *Crust Illuminations* (Murgate, New York, 2012). **Appendix A**.

173   Ettingoff, *Klondyke and his People*, op. cit. **Figure 5.**

174   Most of these interviews were themselves, of course, available on websites. See Nagle again for a complete listing.

of the sort I'd just experienced. In case after case, "permission" had led to exhilaration, and exhilaration, when nostrils turned up empty, to the sort of despair I'd known that morning. In other words, few were those who passed the First Gate without sooner or later meeting the Second. PED was less the exception than the rule.

I should note that, for one significant reason, the disappointment experienced by Klondyke's subjects was probably greater than my own. Though initially funded by the National Institute of Health,[175] his research had benefited from another stroke of good fortune when a ready supply of Rhinobate, the drug I'd just come upon in my Internet search, was donated by the

Figure 5   Maggie Ettingoff.

Costa Rican Rain Forest Foundation. Ettingoff (**Figure 5**) explained that Rhinobate grew wild, like a spore, in the shade of Sabal Palmetto Palm trees in the Corcovado rain forest, in southern Costa Rica. On inhalation, it produced "significant"[176] and "extremely irritating"[177] crusts, called "rhinobatoids," within twelve minutes. Its use in picking rituals by the Coribundi, who were native to the forest, had been documented by Haggerty and other anthropologists. It's no surprise that Klondyke considered the Costa Rican donation the turning point in his research. It had made possible, for the first time, controlled extraction studies. Since rhinobatoids were particularly dense

---

175   See Grants/History/NIH.com for a record of this original grant.

176   Ettingoff, *Klondyke and his People*, op. cit., 68.

177   Ibid.

and aggressive, it also produced a kind of PED which was even darker than that which I'd experienced that morning.

For Ettingoff, however, PED was not an obstacle but

> "a breakthrough which reminds us, every time it occurs, that Nasalism is not a goal-oriented act. Picking is but a small component of this practice. Important though it is, the excitement of extraction can be somewhat distracting. In fact, it is precisely the transience of extraction-euphoria that makes Nasalism, in the end, transformative. The despair we feel in the aftermath of extraction is nothing less than its ultimate affirmation."[178]

I don't know that I completely grasped the meaning of these words but epiphany is not too strong a word for their immediate effect on me. With barely a pause for reflection, I opened my word processor and copied them into the blog I'd begun before Sara's IM arrived. Less than an hour later it was on her computer, and soon after that, uploaded. Needless to say, I also sent it, with a note of gratitude, to Ettingoff herself, whose email address I found on her website.

[178]   Ibid., 234.

FIVE

I'd just uploaded the blog when the telephone rang. It was George again, calling on his cell from the treadmill at the clinic. Much though we'd kept in touch, I was surprised to hear his voice. Restricting himself to email and IMs, he'd not once telephoned since his breakdown. In fact, I think very few people, outside his immediate family and, of course, the doctors and nurses at the clinic, had heard his voice in the last two years.

I heard his feet pounding on the treadmill and the voice of an anchorman from the television overhead. "Tell me one thing," he said. "Are you serious or fucking with my head?"

"About what?"

"C'mon, Wally. No games, okay? The blog! I just read it. Are you for real or is this a novel?"

"What do you think?"

"In other words, you don't know what the fuck you're talking about!"

Short of breath from running, his words clipped by quick inhalations, he sounded a whole lot better than the last time I'd heard his voice – on "Oprah." But almost two years had passed since then, of course. At the time of that interview, he was reeling from his time in the White House, a term which had ended with the lowest – by ten points – "approval rating" of any president in history. Heavily medicated and, by his own estimation, suicidal, he'd so lacked animation then that even his enemies expressed compassion for him.[179]

"Come on, Wally, level with me! No games this morning, okay? I'm too fucked up. I haven't read anything in years that fucked me up like this, and God knows I was fucked up enough before I started. At first, I took it for a joke but suddenly it hit me. Oh my God! He aint kidding! 'Fucked up' is an understatement, man. Dizzy's more like it. Sick to my fucking stomach! I'm thinking, 'This is horseshit. I never read anything so disgusting,' but I aint completely sure. What's he want? I thought. Laughter? Anger? Shit, maybe he just wants to fuck me up! Hang on. I've got to take this call."

The anchorman gave way to commercials. Toothpaste, as I recall, an SUV, prostate medication. When he returned, his voice was confidential. "Okay, I admit it. I'm a picker from way back! Fucking addicted, to be honest about it. Thirty seconds to spare, that's where I go. Thirty? Shit, try ten! Five! But just like you, a hypocrite. Hide behind the newspaper, run to the bathroom, anything to hide. Ashamed, embarrassed, you know what I mean. Don't rock the boat! Christ, I don't even look in the mirror! God forbid Laura should see. Who am I kidding? Please, God, tell me why am I such a wimp! Oh shit, hang on a second, okay?"

A moment later, he went on where he'd left off. "But lemme tell you something, pal. You turned me loose! This morning was like the first time. No bullshit, no holding back! How they say it in Nashville? 'Pickin' and grinning!' Like I never done it before! A long slow pick that lit me up. And what a feeling when I got it! Sweet all over! And now? Just like you wrote! On top, no fear, got a chance again! I aint saying I'm ready for Laura, but I swear to God I turned the corner! Not a sign of depression and I aint even took my pills!"

---

179 Reviews of "Oprah" interview.

He pounded and panted for a moment, then had to interrupt again. "Sorry, Wally. This is the wife. Got to sign off. Glad I got you though. Had to say thanks. I know I can't be sure but I swear to God I feel like you've saved my life."

✹✹✹✹

Tuesday lunch was a ritual with Sara. Unless one of us was out of town, we met every week, in the Executive Dining Room at the Murgate building.

Heading uptown in a taxi I worked on my BlackBerry and at the same time – idly,[180] as one does with crusts of that size – on something between a 5 and a 6. No surprise there. As we know from various fields of research – rhinology, pulmonology, meterology, not to mention, since we're dealing here with urban experience, sociology – no environment generates nasal secretion like stop-and-go traffic in the polluted air of big cities. Traffic was heavy that morning so I had plenty of time. On the back of the driver's seat was a video screen which offered commercials and, by way of buttons on the touch-screen, ten different channels: News, sports, MTV, ESPN, YouTube, and an on-demand feature for prime-time shows, classic boxing, football, and basketball. One could pay for one's choices and, for that matter, one's ride by swiping a credit card in a slot at the bottom of the screen. Fortunately, the screen was one that (unlike many) allowed an on-off option, so I got rid of it quickly. I had still to deal, however, with the driver's music. He was a young Latino with a pony tail, playing rock, very loud, on a pair of speakers which happened to be just inches from my ears. It was hard to get through to him because he was also on

---

180   Those who follow Rhinotillexis.com will know that at the first conference on Nasalism at MIT, I disagreed with Klondyke when (in his otherwise insightful paper, "Nasalism in Motion") he likened such idleness to the dissociation of PreNasalism. See Volume 1 of *Extract* – June, 2009 – the annual report of the International Academy of Nasalism, for report on our discussion as well as a transcript of the paper itself.

his cell phone, but when finally I managed, he was cordial and agreeable.

"Is it rock that bothers you or music in general?"

"Just rock at the moment," I said.

"How about jazz or classical?" he said. "I'm on my iPod. How about bluegrass or country? No? Coltrane? Dylan? Mozart?"

"Bach?"

"Sure."

"Cello suites?"

"Casals? Starker?"

We settled on Casals, so I returned to my BlackBerry in reasonable comfort, insulated from the outside world. I checked my voice mail, then my email, then responses to the blog, then clicked on the Internet. I went first to YouTube and – as I'd promised myself since I'd first heard of it – the video of Peggy Ann Taylor's scandalous pick on MTV. At least six different versions had been uploaded, and each of them included anywhere from half a dozen to fifty "discussions" offering the predictable range of opinions – "disgusting,"

Figure 6   Peggy Ann Taylor, at the instant which *Time Magazine* called "the death of a taboo" and *USA Today*, "the death of television." Though a lifelong practitioner, Taylor says of this moment that it was "completely spontaneous, an act of my body, not my mind."

"courageous," "gorgeous," "silly," etc. Tall, darkhaired, and slightly goofy, her exuberant insertion was accompanied by a defiant extension of her tongue. I watched the clip twice, scanned the discussions, then clicked onto Rhinotillexis.com. There were a number of new links listed. While I wandered among them, traffic slowed until finally it backed up altogether at 34th Street. As horns honked on all sides, I found my way to a Wiki on "mucus" and, by means of a link it suggested, the world-renowned Mucus Lab of Israeli scientist Tamar Dror, at Technion, in Tel Aviv. Strange to say, given the research I'd done already, Dror was the first to make me appreciate the role the cilia played in crust-metabolism.

> "Cilia are threadlike cells that wave back and forth over some of the surface tissue. They help keep the nasal passageways clear of particulate matter. From time to time, and especially in the winter, the mucus dries out, begins to get 'gloopy' or gluelike. That slows down the cilia. A virus can stop the cilia altogether. When the cilia stop waving, secretions pool in the back of the nose. The consistency thickens and suddenly you're aware of an annoying presence, somewhere in the nostril, that demands to be removed."[181]

I bookmarked Dror, then followed a link to legal historian Flannery Baum and her extraordinary work on anti-picking laws.[182] Finally, a link at Baum's website led me to Aldous Prezl, the chemical engineer from the University of Stockholm, whose passion for picking, according to the profile on his site, had led him to study rhinology as an avocation. As most of us know, Prezl was the first to explore, measure, and develop equations relating the chemical and environmental variables which influence crust adhesion, to the nostril on its inner surface and, of course, to the fingertip on its outer.[183] His new work, as I discovered now, further refined these equations to include what he called "the power struggle" between internal and external adhesion "which in every case will determine the success

---

181 Dror, Tamar. "The Hysteries of Cilia," *Annals of Otolaryngology* Vol. 217 (April 2007) 235–241.

182 Baum, Flannery. *Legislating Taboo* (Omaha, Nebraska: Lester, Link and Goforth, 1998). Among other sad tales, Baum reports the first legal prohibition of nose-picking, a Memphis, Tennessee, edict, in 1936, which made "public picking" a misdemeanor, punishable by a $50 fine.

183 Prezl, Aldous. *Nasal Adhesion* (Boise, Idaho: University of Idaho Press, 2000).

or failure of extraction."[184] Of all I found on my search that morning, it was Prezl's work which most intrigued me. Fortunately, my BlackBerry had word-processing software, so I was able to copy the summary of his article and email it to my home computer and, of course, to Carlotta, who would organize and file it. If you've read *The Complete Book of Nasalism*, you know that Prezl would become a significant figure in our practice.[185] Clarissa Ponte, the inventor of Merck's inhaler, Rhinonex, which is said to produce crusts that rival rhinobatoids in glucosity, calls Prezl's work central to her own.[186] Carlos Rodriguez, one of the more prominent anti-nasal psychologists, who postulates that the passion for nose-picking derives entirely from what he calls "the inherent adhesive capacity of an individual's secretions,"[187] credits Prezl's equations in every article he's published.

Traffic moved a bit but gridlocked again ten blocks from the Murgate building, at 47th Street and 3rd Avenue. A digital display on the roof of a taxi to our left showed basketball scores. On our right, a bus with a bright digital sign advertised an upcoming Barbara Kruger show at the Mary Boone Gallery in Chelsea. Interspersed with its copy, it flashed two versions of her famous "Battleground" series – *Your Body is a Battleground* and its even more famous variation, *Your Nose is a Battleground* (**Figure 7**), which would soon become an emblem for our movement.[188] Year after year, T-shirts and buttons featuring

---

184   Ibid., 2.

185   Linchak, *The Complete Book of Nasalism*, op. cit., 236–239.

186   Ponte, Clarissa. Clarrissaponte.com, January 24, 2011. See the *Merck Journal* Vol. 234 (May 2011) 38–45 for a description of Ponte's research and the initial announcement of Rhinonex.

187   Rodriguez, Carlos. "Mucoid Adhesion and OCD," *The Annals of Rhinology* Vol. 21 (August 2011) 13–20.

188   See the cover of *Rhinotillexis Updated* (New York: Murgate, 2012) and page 234 of *The Complete Book of Nasalism*.

Figure 7   Barbara Kruger, *Your Nose is a Battleground*.

Many believe that this painting is autobiographical, an affirmation of Kruger's Nasalism (see "Kruger Picks" by Jason Karmody, *New York Magazine*, April 10, 2009, and "Kruger's Nose," *Art in America*, January 2010), but while taking no position for or against the practice (see "Kruger Laughs," *New York Times*, April 16, 2009), Kruger denies that she picks and resents the suggestion that there is literal connection between her life and her work. A careful study of the Kruger literature supports her in this regard. See *Kruger* (New York: Abrams, 2009) 61–63, and the catalog of her recent show at New York's Museum of Modern Art, page 102. All doubt, surely, was removed when the Mary Boone Gallery, despite the fact that it represents Kruger, did not include her in "Nasalism – A Group Show," in June 2013.

this image outsell all others at our conferences and on our websites.

As traffic eased, I completed my extraction. Small though it was, and ichorous, it was not uninteresting. How often has it been noted that the intensity of a twinge is not entirely dependent on the size and texture of a crust? Here was a case in which insignificant volume and close to unqualified liquidity produced sensation of thrilling intensity. Had I spent more time on his website that morning, I'd have seen that Prezl, factoring environment and air pollution into his adhesion equations, explains this as well. No one who's studied him will be surprised to find that twinges deepen in heavy traffic, especially (since nothing affects adhesion more than one's immediate environment) if experienced in the back seat of a taxi.

Arriving at the Murgate building, I closed my BlackBerry, paid the driver, and entered the lobby. I was quickly aware that George was not the only one who'd read my blog. Ahead of me in the revolving door was Executive Editor Ellen Frick. A tall grey-haired African-American woman in her early sixties, she was an avid reader of my work who sent me long, thoughtful, and sometime critical emails about anything she read, including the blog.

"Careful, Wally," she said. "It's a great metaphor, but it'll weigh the book down. There's no bigger taboo than disgust."

"It's not a metaphor," I said.

"What is it then?"

"I don't know. But trust me, Ellen, it's not a metaphor."

She laughed. "A metaphor then for not-a-metaphor?"

"Not that either," I said.

"The essence, at last, of postmodernism?"

"Who knows?"

"But even the postmodernists don't like disgust!"

"Neither do I."

"Well, it's nothing to joke about, that's for sure."

"I'm not joking."

"I had an uncle, Freddie Boatright, who picked so much he made a hole in his septum. Took surgery to fix it and, from what I hear, his breathing is still a problem. Friend of mine, Chinese fellow named Henry Chang, has a son who got himself addicted. Never stopped! In school, at the dinner table, even in church! Took Ritalin and Zoloft both to get it under control."

Most of the people in editorial hadn't read the blog or at least weren't mentioning it, but the route from editorial to the elevator took me through publicity. That meant a visit with Charlie or, as we called him, "Geek" Williams. Of all the people at Murgate, he was the one I'd most depend on when the book came out. Director of the online department, so-called "Web Master," he was a thirty-year-old who'd once been a hacker with less-than-legal skills and an outlaw reputation on the web.[189] He'd been hired at Murgate, at the age of nineteen, for his spam and virus expertise. Like me, he was close to the Bush family. Karl Rove, as well. Indeed, there were rumors that he'd played a significant role in the elections of 2000 and 2004, designing the programs which, as most everyone knew by now, had hacked into Florida and Ohio voting machines to swing the vote to the Republicans. One of a new breed of publicists who understood viral marketing, his career had been as meteoric as Sara's. Though he worked our side of the street now, he'd never abandoned his hacking instincts and, over the years, as the Internet had come to dominate sales and promotion, he'd become a major weapon for almost every company (forty-seven at last count) in the Murgate stable. Expert in "search engine optimization," he could push most any product or label to the top of search-results on Google, Yahoo, or any other. Using boilerplates and macros he'd developed, he maintained more than twenty blogs of his own, and he was said to be the best in

---

[189] See Herohacker.com and the favorite among the many blogs which Geek maintained, Ctwilliamsalone.com.

the industry at planting video-publicity on sites like YouTube, FaceBook, and MySpace, placing reviews on booksellers like Amazon and Barnes and Noble, and of course, disseminating email publicity which circumvented anti-spam filters. It was also rumored that he used botnet programs to take over private, unprotected computers and use them as "zombies" to publicize the whole range of Murgate products. His most recent inspiration, which he'd confessed to Sara and me over dinner one night, was a program with which, using what he called "chat viruses," he could plant subjects in chat room conversations and keep them going on their own.

Small and wiry, hair unkempt and shoulder-length, Geck looked like a teenager. He wore small oval-shaped, un-rimmed spectacles, black jeans with ragged cuffs, a grey hooded sweatshirt and high-top black basketball shoes. As usual, he did not bother to say hello. "Nose-picking!" he cried. "Fuck me! Stuff like that is what the web lives for. If I can't move this along, I ought to be in another profession. I've already written it into a couple of chat rooms. Your blog is already number three on Yahoo. Tomorrow you'll be number one there as well as Google."

The dining room was an elegant penthouse on the 67th floor. Designed, like the building itself, by Frank Ghery, it had been featured in *Architecture Digest*, *Design International*, *The New York Times Magazine*, *New York Magazine*, and, for its restaurant, *Gourmet Magazine*, Foodnet.com, and the cable show called "Cooks of the World." It was on the cover of both the most recent Ghery coffee-table book and the "21st Century Architecture" CD-ROM which *Aperture* had published the year before, and, of course, it had been featured in the portrait of Ghery which had appeared two years before on PBS's *American Masters*. It had a solarium skylight, self-service salad and sushi bars, and floor-to-ceiling windows offering full-circle views of Manhattan. Four video monitors, linked to Murgate satellites, hung from the ceiling above the sushi bar. One was tuned to

Murgate's news channel, one to a soccer game between two Murgate teams (England's Manchester United and Mexico's Guadalajara), one offered music videos without sound from another Murgate subsidiary, MTV, and one showed basketball, a replay of a recent game between the Boston Celtics and the New York Knicks, a team which Murgate had owned since its acquisition, four years before, of Madison Square Garden. News headlines ran at the bottom of each screen above another line of stock market and weather updates.

Sara was waiting at a corner table, windows behind her offering up both sides of downtown New York. Sitting across from her, I could see the Lower East Side over her left shoulder, the Lower West Side over her right. Sunlight streaked her hair and blinded me until I leaned a bit and found some shade in front of her face. She was beautiful as ever, but I'd never seen her so agitated. Shifting back and forth between astonishment and confidence, her eyes were luminous, her laugh too frequent and too loud, her hands nervous on the table, and, what was really uncharacteristic, something I'd not seen since our first weeks together, she couldn't stop kissing and chewing on my fingers.

She shook her head with amazement. "Tell me, please, what's going on. I swear to God I've never felt like this before."

Quoting from her memoir, where she devotes an entire chapter to this period in her life, Leiter cites the transformation she was experiencing as an example of the "bipolarity and hysteria which Nasalism commonly induces."[190] I doubt that even he would disagree, however, with Crimmins' assertion, in his *New Yorker* review of the same memoir, that no one has equaled her for describing "the energy released when the nose-picking taboo is challenged and defeated."[191]

"Out of nowhere?" she went on. "In a limo? I thought I was

190   Leiter, *Nasalism and Manic Depression*, op. cit., 125.

191   Crimmins, David. "Martinson's Truth," *The New Yorker (*April 23, 2012) 77–78.

hallucinating. But oh my God how deep it was. Even in the early days with you, I never came like that."

The waiter arrived with the usual executive perks – bowls of edamame and seaweed salad, a large bottle of Pellegrino. He offered champagne as well, but both of us declined.

Sara squeezed my hand again. "Saki?"

"No thanks."

"Sushi?"

"Thanks. I'm not hungry."

"You? Not hungry?"

"No," I said, and then, with a kind of amazement, realizing for the first time what we've come to see as a common effect of the Post Extraction Despair from which I was still suffering. "Not much appetite today."[192]

She put my thumb in her mouth and sucked it. In her memoir, she is explicit about the way in which the practice, "loosening my mind," made such behavior, for the first time in her life, "not just possible but irresistible."

"You fucking bastard," she said, and then, repeating what I'd said without realizing it, "you saw what I was blind to. You took me to the bottom, the root of my fear. Of course I had to vomit."

She said she'd "practiced" three times in her office that morning, twice with "success" and once without. "Blind!" she said again. "I was hiding in the house, gazing through the window, afraid to go out. Afraid of what? Please, God, tell me – afraid of what! Well, it's obvious, isn't it? This is not just about finger and nose. It's about fear and inhibition, conditioning, the tyranny of habit. Vanity! Challenge disgust and you challenge everything that's timid and weak and superficial in yourself!"

She touched her nose with the half-forefinger on her right hand, allowed it brief entry, then quickly withdrew and waved it

---

192   See Orloff, Hallie. "PED and Appetite," *Extract* Vol. 16 May 2012: 20–25.

between us. "All your buttons pushed by crossing this barrier? Come off it! I thought. How can it be? But why should we be surprised? This one inhibition is all inhibition! You cross the inside-outside barrier. The public-private barrier. The good taste-bad taste barrier. Most of all, the mind-body barrier. Who wouldn't freak out? Even before I came, I felt a buzz. Carefree and reckless, almost stoned. Again and again, I'm thinking, 'Finger in your nose, what's the big deal?' Thinking, thinking, trying to understand, but then I see its power is exactly in the fact that it can't be understood! Like you said, it's beyond thought! All your life, you do what you can understand because understanding – especially for a Radcliffe girl like me! – is safety and control! Safety and control is exactly what you give up when you break through this barrier!"

She reached across the table and put her finger in my nose. Just at the tip, the length of a fingernail, but the effect was like connection to a power-source. I felt a pulse run through me, quick sensations in my face, my neck and shoulders, finally my cock. She pushed higher. For the first time, it occurred to me that she'd gone a little crazy, but only, of course, with appreciation.

"What is this?" she said. "Tell me, please, what is this? Not an idea, for sure! Not the words you label it with! Not words! Not description! You put your finger in your nose – that's it! For once in your life, your body is free of your head! Of course it can't be understood!"

SIX

Mickey called on my cell a few minutes after I said goodbye to Sara. Like George, he'd read my blog when it first appeared and, again like George, he wasn't altogether sure if I'd meant to be taken seriously. "Let's talk," he said, "while it's fresh in my mind. How about coffee this afternoon?"

We met later at our usual place, an espresso bar in his neighborhood. It wasn't his style to make a point slowly, and he didn't hesitate now. Waiting outside when I arrived, he said, "Differentiation. That's the bottom line, isn't it?"

He'd always said that eating kept psychoanalysts in business, and he was an advertisement for his theory. He looked to have added pounds since our last meeting, two weeks before. It didn't help that he wore his pants so low that his belly hung over his belt. One of his shirt buttons was open in the vicinity of his navel, and he wasn't wearing an undershirt. His stained, wrinkled shirt was a blue button-down, his tie a black-and-white polka dot, his jacket the ragged brown corduroy he'd worn in college twenty years before.

The coffee shop was small – six round marble tables, French café chairs, and a tiny counter for a cash register and a tray of pastries in front of an elaborate brass espresso machine. The TV above the cash register showed golf without sound and, as in the Murgate dining room, headlines, stock quotes, and weather reports scrolling at the bottom of the screen. Empty except for us, the room was saturated with the smell of coffee. The hit from it was like the hit from caffeine itself. Charged as we sat down, I was reminded of Sunday mornings in bed with Sara and more explicitly, last Sunday morning, the breakthrough crust, its burst of energy so much like caffeine's.[193] It wasn't the first time I'd associated Nasalism and caffeine. I was thinking metaphorically but it wouldn't be long before brain-scans from Klondyke's and other rhinology labs confirmed that such effects were neurochemical.[194]

Settling into his chair, Mickey took two BlackBerrys from his pocket and placed them side by side on the table. On the left was an old black one he used for practice-related business, on the right, a new red one he reserved for what he liked to call his "show business career."

"Don't think you discovered the wheel," he said. "Later today I'll email you at least six articles you should read. Three of them by me. *The Journal of Obsessive-Compulsive Disorder*[195] four years ago, *Lacan Journal*[196] last year, and, just a few months ago – did you see it? – *Psychology Today*.[197] The first was more or less traditional. Narcissism, masturbation, self-hate objectified, etcetera, etcetera. Boilerplate. I went deeper in *Lacan* but deeper

---

193 Needless to say, many researchers have related Nasalism and caffeine. Among the many interesting articles on the subject, I recommend Ettingoff's "Energy and Extraction" which first appeared on her website and has recently been published in her essay collection, *Nasalism My Way* (New York: Murgate, 2018).

194 Klondyke, Marcus. "The Neurochemistry of Rhinotillexis," *Scientific American* September 2012: 103–110.

195 Linchak, Mickey. "Compulsive Nosepicking," *The Journal of Obsessive-Compulsive Disorder* Vol. 234 (April 2004) 66–72.

196 Linchak, Mickey. "Physical Narcissism," *Lacan Journal* Vol. 201 (August 2008) 87–90.

197 Linchak, Mickey. "Masturbation and its Derivatives," *Psychology Today* August 2009: 11–20.

still in *Psychology Today*. I'm still getting letters on that piece."

All these papers, of course, were available on his website, which also offered streams of his cable show as well as DVDs for sale. A collection of his monographs was under contract at Columbia University Press but his TV show had elicited interest from trade publishers and, having signed on with my agent, Peter Conrad, he was circulating a proposal for what Peter called a self-help book and what he himself called "a combination diary-notebook. Intimate notes, in other words, of a psychoanalyst at work." Offering surprisingly deep therapeutic guidance to those who called, his TV show had maintained a primetime slot and won fairly decent, and improving, ratings for the three years he'd been on the air. According to Personaldownload.net, it was also popular on YouTube. There were those who thought he owed his success to his name, which is to say, his connection to me, but of course I had nothing to do with it. He had what Rebecca Powell, TV critic of *The Wall Street Journal*, called "the charisma of zero-charisma." Dressed in the same sloppy garb he wore now, fidgeting in his chair and – interjecting phrases like "the notion that" or "so to speak" – much more self-conscious and verbose than anyone you'd ever seen on television, he looked completely out of place on camera, but as Powell wrote, "in a world of slick media, a dose of Dr. Mickey is a dose of vitamins."[198]

The waitress brought us menus. Scanning his, Mickey said, "It started with mother, didn't it? Remember her face when we picked? Twisted, ghoulish, lips pursed like she'd smelled a fart? Remember? Like any minute she's gonna vomit? Wasn't that fucking beautiful? Made me want to pick forever! All your life you fight the umbilical cord, and bang, you cut it with a booger! Show me anything makes a kid feel better than making mommy puke."

---

198 Powell, Rebecca. "Dr. Mickey to the Rescue," *The Wall Street Journal* June 12, 2007: 45–47.

He put down his menu and bent over the BlackBerry he used for his practice. Leaning close, eyes just inches from the screen, he used his thumbs to type out a note for himself. "Your blog is simplistic but it gave me insights. I started a new paper right after I finished it. Maybe I can help you. You're onto something, Wally, but you aren't there yet. As usual, you're too literary. Trapped in language, that's another cord you've got to cut. Listen: every booger is your dick! That's the bottom line. Cock and balls and autonomy, everything she tried to destroy. Make her squirm, make her puke! I'll send you the paper when I'm done. Every pick takes you out of the womb! That's where I start in *Lacan*. Nothing brings a child to life like disgust on his mother's face! Think about it! Why else do we pick the minute we finish fucking? Isn't it logical? I don't know about you but I'm into my nose as soon as I pull out. Every woman is your mother! Black Holes that trap you, that's what they are, and boogers get you out! Trust me, Wally. You're onto something deep!"

"I don't do it after fucking."

"I don't believe you."

"No, I really don't."

"A guy who dissociates as much as you do – why should I trust your memory?"

The waitress took our order. Cappuccino for him, espresso for me, a plate of biscotti shared. A moment later we heard the whine of the grinder and the roar of the steamer on the espresso machine. Feeling lethargic, as often when I was with him, I went to the bathroom and washed my face with cold water. Stared into the mirror, looked deep in my eyes, put my finger in my nose. No crust calling, no discomfort, nothing to search out or extract, but there it was, the energy again. Not quite what Klondyke calls "crust-awakening"[199] or Fawck,

---

199   Klondyke, *Rhinotillexis*, op. cit., 235.

"subject-object unification,"[200] but I felt much better when I came back to the table.

Mickey liked cinnamon on his cappuccino. Sprinkling freely, he ate with his other hand, biting into his cookie and talking, as always, while he chewed. "But why are you so categorical? You're always that way! Nothing scares you like ambiguity. Black and white, either or, nothing in between! It's the secret of your success, isn't it? The sort of readers you collect, ambiguity freaks them out. Especially these days, they want everything packaged, tied up and explained, like the evening news. What's the buzz-word? Closure! No wonder you're a superstar! But look at the hole it puts you in! Where's the paradox? The depth? The reality? What are you afraid of? You can't outsmart dependency! If mother's disgust is the key to your balls, you'll always be emasculated. Wake up, sweetheart! It's time to be honest. Nose-picking is regression! Your blog is total fucking narcissism. Me, me, me. What you want is endless masturbation! You call it autonomy but what you're really after is to merge with mommy again."

"I don't call it autonomy."

He sipped his coffee. "All your life you've had an S&M relationship with mom. You've got power over her, sure. You pick your nose, you spank her. Hurt her. Make her puke! It's like crack or heroin. Sure-fire, immediate, quintessential high, right? No, sweetheart. Wrong! You've got it backward. Your balls are in her pocket! You're powerless without her! She controls you with her disgust, cuts off your dick by puking! Wrong, Wally, wrong! Power is within! You've got to annihilate her once and for all! No matter how you slice it, dependency does you in. Finish with nose-picking or it will finish with you."

Coffee always did this to him. Thought alone could get him high but in combination with caffeine, it made him incoherent.

---

200   Fawck, Robert. Rfawck.com, October 2, 2011.

"Have you read Winnicott?"

"Some," I said.

"Derrida?"

"It's been a while."

"Wittgenstein?"

"Of course."

"What's with your voice? Got a cold?"

"No."

"Watch it, okay? You don't sound like yourself. You depressed?"

"Less than in a long time."

"Sleeping well?"

"For the last few days, yeah."

"Well, watch it, okay. Ideas like this – they do you in. At root, they're regressive. You can't jerk off forever. Sure it's okay to pick now and then, but it's a halfway house, not a destination. Be careful, okay? I hear it in your voice. Something weak, passive. Hints of collapse and disintegration, to be honest about it. Talk to me, okay? Anytime. I was worried when I read the blog, but I'm a lot more worried now."

He took another sip of coffee, then another bite of biscotti, then talked again while his mouth was full. "But don't get me wrong. There's nothing wrong with picking! It depends on how you relate to it. Honor it, respect it – okay! Fix on it and you've got yourself addicted. Face up to the need is what you've got to do. Free it from dependency! Then, who knows… maybe it will help you. Morbid dependency, that's what you're flirting with. No wonder you're depressed. You're totally addicted to a mother who couldn't let go! Why else were you always such a good boy? She's your real booger! It's her you have to pick! She wanted to devour you! Couldn't stand that you were breathing on your own! I'm not talking habit. I'm talking emasculation! She's your heroin and picking is your methadone! Get rid of both, Walker. Then – pick or don't pick. It won't matter which!"

He sipped again and swallowed the last of his biscotti. His lips were dotted with crumbs and, as always when he chewed, the click of his teeth when he bit down was audible, strident. Eating was not an act of leisure for him. Bites or swallows followed each other so quickly that his hands, moving back and forth between mouth and food or cup, seemed to be on springs. He bent over his BlackBerry and typed again.

I said, "You're addicted to that thing, aren't you?"

"Yeah," he said, still typing. "It's my booger." And then, "It always helps to talk to you. I'm getting clear. I'll finish the paper tonight. The thing about picking – it has to be forbidden. It doesn't work if it's not disgusting. Disgust is what gets you off. Always has. You've been a good boy all your life, but you're bad when you pick. What's gonna happen if now you make it respectable? Where's the disgust? As usual, you're trapped in contradiction. Rejecting mom and dad but explaining why you do it! Hoping they'll understand, give you permission to reject them. What's the use if they permit it? The real trap is explanation! Language! Your blog is a perfect description of the depression and passivity, the total fucking pathological narcissism that most writers suffer from. It ought to be published in our journal. But you've got to go deeper, take it to the bottom line. Where's my balls? That's what you're asking. A woman who likes to be spanked – what do you get from spanking her?"

"Maybe a lot," I said.

"Yeah? Maybe so. But any way you slice it, it's a swamp. What's S&M if not a swamp for top and bottom both? Like nose-picking. Anti-depressants. Heroin. You sure you're not depressed? That's not your voice at all."

I thought for a moment to tell him about the Founder, this odd excitement I continued to feel, even now, when I heard his voice in my head, not to mention when I took dictation from him. "I'm not depressed," I said.

"It's a contradiction, I know. You need to separate but you're still her child. After all, you started in her womb. There's no escaping that. That's cause and effect! So here's the thing: pick because you want to! Wholeheartedly! Once you feel it, deep inside – I want to pick! – you're autonomous, differentiated. Totally free of her! You don't give a fuck if it disgusts her or not. It's only when we accept the circularity of our minds that we begin to move straight ahead! You're free of cause and effect because for once in your life you accept it. Come on! It's obvious! Brush up on your Buddhism!"

He looked at his watch. "Shit, I've got a patient in fifteen minutes." He waved to the waitress and – writing in the air – asked for the check. "Another writer, passive and depressed, emasculated by his mother and his wife, just like you. Ten years of treatment and no improvement whatsoever."

"Why don't you cut him loose then?"

"He couldn't make it without me."

"And you talk about addiction?"

"What do you mean?"

"Get him picking. Maybe he'll be free of you."

"Why not?" he laughed. "I'll get him to read your blog!"

He pocketed his BlackBerrys but quickly took out the red one again. "These are good notes," he said. "You might be interested in them." He pressed some buttons and a moment later I heard the beeping sound that announced connection to the Internet. "I'll email them to you now, okay?"

SEVEN

Back at my office, I had time at last to deal with response to the blog. It came in the form of direct email to me and to the blog itself as well as to my own and (responding to its publication in *MurgateLive*) Murgate's websites. There was also of course snail mail – from the Postal Service, FedEx, and UPS. The greater part of it was unrelated to the blog. Today, it was more or less typical – eleven manuscripts and six sets of galleys asking for blurbs, plus six published books sent by editors, publishers, or the writers themselves in the hope that I might review, recommend, or mention them in my blog. Of this total – twenty-three – three were written by friends and four by former students. The rest, in all probability, had found my address on the Internet. The days when one could hide out from this sort of thing had disappeared when websites like Phonebook.com came online.

My personal email box (its address also available online) had more than fifty messages (in addition, of course, to more than two hundred spam which my anti-spam filter picked up), my website more than eighty, the blog more than sixty. Needless to say, no small number of these came with attachments or photographs or links to articles or videos. The level of response varied. The great majority were personal attacks – from parents who felt I was encouraging their kids' habits, from those, like J.J. Lundy and others from the so-called "Booger Blogs," who accused me of betraying the habit by making it respectable, and at least four who'd written about the habit in their own blogs and accused me of plagiarizing. Others were interesting, even valuable. One email came from the Turkish otolaryngologist, Oram Balakian. While he appreciated my blog, he said, he felt that I needed to examine "the molecular composition of mucus and its relation to the sinus cavities."[201]

There were also commercial responses. Peter Conrad, my agent, forwarded five proposals – two for books and three for articles – on nose-picking. Geek Williams forwarded fifty-six messages, culled, he explained, from a total of more than 1,700 which had come to the magazine and several hundred to the company website. Scanning quickly, I set aside what had to be read at once and sent the rest to Carlotta, who would, as usual, filter out what I needed to read or answer and attend to the rest on her own. Sara's secretary, Connie James, sent the first batch of search-results turned up by Sara's research staff. Among other things, it included thirty-six websites and a treasure trove of academic and literary material which was directly or indirectly connected to research or discussion about the habit. Some had turned up on my search that morning, but the bulk of it was new to me.

Characteristically, Sara had come up with websites so exotic that I could not resist them. Trigeminal.com, for example, was centered on the work of Barry Fitzgibbon, at the University of New Zealand, who, according to his anything but modest home page, was "the world's greatest authority on the trigeminal nerve" (**Figure 8**). In addition to summarizing his research and, of course, listing his articles, books, grants, and degrees, the site included several links to research on "trigeminal rhinology." The first of these summarized data on excitation of the

---

201 Balakian returned to this point at the First Annual Nasalism Conference at MIT in 2010. Though expressing great appreciation for my blog, he was categorical in his assertion that I needed to examine "the molecular composition of mucus and its relation to the sinus cavities."

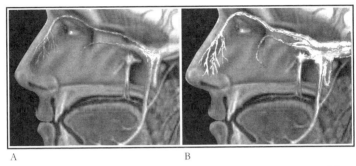

A   B

Figure 8   Rhinomag images of the trigeminal nerve, produced by Barry Fitzgibbon, at the University of New Zealand. Figure A shows a patient with no significant crust development, thus minimal activation of the nerve; Figure B, an extremely tenacious 7.6 which, in Klondyke's memorable phrase, is "screaming for attention."

nasal membrane. The second was the website of Rockefeller University's Rhinology Department, where its then-chief, Janis Hartley, a formidable researcher with more than three hundred papers published under his name, was using Fitzgibbon's data to investigate sensations generated by crusts or what he called "mucosal irritation."[202]

As I was exploring Connie's attachments, an IM from Geek appeared on-screen. He wanted me to see the first Technorati.com figures on my blog. Though its 6,274 hits were nowhere near enough to put it on Technorati.com's "current hit parade," it was already listed among the "notables."

I was just about to answer him when an IM from George appeared.

---

202   Hartley, of course, is best known for his disturbing article, "Quantification of the Nasal Membrane," *The New England Journal of Medicine* August 2010: 121–130. More than any other research, I think, it inspired the formidable anti-nasal view that our practice is strictly, as he maintains, "a function of anatomy." Offering what he calls "quantifiable proof" that the number of "nasal nerve endings differs significantly from individual to individual," it is his belief that "rhinotillexic passion is directly proportional to the number of nerve endings in the nasal membrane and/or the conductive capacity of the trigeminal nerve, thus causing objects in the nose to be more or less irritating, the need to extract more or less desperate and irresistible."

"You there?"

"Yeah," I typed. "'Sup?"

"More same!"

"????"

"No medication. Four picks today. Each better than one before. What can I tell you? Feel like president again."

Given the countless theories which have been advanced to explain the transformation he was going through – which would soon, of course, once he announced it on "Larry King Live," be widely reported and endlessly discussed in the media – it is audacious to grant supremacy to one, but in my view, Klondyke's (on various news outlets but, most cogently on NPR's "All Things Considered," June 16, 2008) was by far the most insightful. Certainly, it was the most scientific. Produced as it was through the new brain-scan technology he and Fawck had developed at MIT, his data confirmed what had long been suspected – that in addition to the trigeminal nerve, almost any extraction (especially those which are "Nasal" rather than "PreNasal") can affect neurochemical metabolism, specifically serotonin uptake. In other words, such effect paralleled that of the anti-depressant George had been taking.

He signed off without saying goodbye, so I went back to my snail mail. It included three DVDs – from her agent, its producer, and Peggy Ann Taylor herself – of the extraction I'd seen earlier on YouTube; two copies – one from its producer and one from Jerry Seinfeld himself – of the famous nose-picking episode on his show; and a package from Klondyke's publisher containing a press packet of his reviews, the galleys of a new article, soon to be published in *The Annals of Rhinology*,[203] and, most important, a brochure for the historic conference – "Rhinotillexis: a Body-Mind Symposium" – which

---

[203] Klondyke, Marcus. "Rhinotillexis and the Amygdala" *The Annals of Rhinology* Vol. 383 (April 2011) 42–51. A shorter version of the same article appeared in *Scientific American*'s "Nose and Brain" issue, August 2012.

was scheduled to take place the following summer, at MIT, where he'd recently become a professor.

The cover image on the brochure was a small print of the famous Ellen Bernstein photograph of an 8 extracted by Klondyke himself.[204] The brochure was of such historical significance that, as you may know, I include it as Appendix B in *The Complete Book of Nasalism*. A glossy foldout listing three days of meetings, discussion groups, and workshops with photographs and curriculum vitae of its fourteen participants, it featured four people I'd already encountered on the web – Robert Fawck, Denis Haggerty, Lucille Bloch, and Ellen Bernstein – and another half a dozen with whom I'd soon be familiar. In addition to Klondyke's specialty, rhinology, the symposium would cover the neurophilosophy (Fawck), the anthropology (Haggerty), and the biochemistry (Clara Neal Cassidy) of Nasalism. Bloch's classification scale (**Appendix A**) would make its public debut, Janet Greene would present the first of her data on Nasalism and electromagnetism, and Dorothy Patterson would offer a preliminary synopsis of the data she'd collected – surveys in this case of writers and painters – for the book which would offer the first legitimate sociological data on the practice: *Nose-Picking and Creativity*.[205] Within two weeks, noted the brochure, Rhinotillexis.com would post the conference schedule, information on the speakers, an ordering form for the tapes, transcripts, DVD and CD, and, of course, a downloadable PDF of the brochure itself.

As I studied the brochure, there occurred an event no less important than the first of my breakthrough crusts. I had just stood up from my desk. Standing at the window, taking deep breaths, I felt an irritation in my left nostril. Since I'd not had a crust for some time, I was not surprised. The great surprise

204   Bernstein, op. cit.

205   Patterson, Dorothy. *Nose-Picking and Creativity* (New York: Norton, 2012).

was my response to it. Despite the fact that it was clearly or, as some would say, *appropriately*, irritating, I made no move in its direction! At least a 7, maybe an 8, it should have produced impatience to extract, but what I felt was a patience so clear and unequivocal that I could not contest it. Nowhere within myself could I find the aggression and desire which crusts of this size had always evoked.

Thus did I encounter, for the first time, the PostNasal Gap,[206] or what Ettingoff calls our "Third Gate."[207] Though it seldom follows so quickly on the Second (I suspect it did so in my case because I had put so much effort, for the purposes of my third nasal blog, into understanding Post Extraction Despair), it's a rare Nasalist who does not eventually find his way to it. What it has in common with Post Extraction Despair, of course, is *waiting*, but the difference between the two could not be more dramatic. The Second Gate is about *waiting for crusts*, the Third about *waiting itself*. The former is involuntary, an experience dictated by external circumstances, but what I'd just experienced seemed to be, however conflicted, *a matter of choice*. For no reason I could discern, the aggression typically aroused by crusts was replaced by a state of mind that resembled nothing so much as curiosity and, dare I say, equanimity. To my astonishment, I found myself *interested* in the crust and the sensations it was generating. I had no desire to get rid of it or them. We know now, of course, that this is a natural evolution of the practice. Of all the leaps we take, none is more fertile but none, for sure, is more challenging. The first response to the Third Gate is almost always the sort of confusion I now experienced. With regard to my hesitation to pick, I felt a kind of self-doubt which, because it produced neither aggression nor impatience, left me completely unnerved. I suspected

206 Ettingoff, *Nasalism My Way*, op. cit., 124–156.

207 Ibid.

myself of regression, betrayal of the practice, disregard almost cavalier toward the revelations it had produced. Needless to say, it wasn't long (thirty seconds at most, I estimate) before I resumed my habit. My face flushed and perspiration beading on my forehead, I extracted with impatience so extreme that it bordered on ferocity. Then (with the speed and all-inclusiveness that Fawck and other neurorhinologists have demonstrated time and again in recent work) I succumbed to an amnesia which is no less uncommon than the event it occluded. Weeks would pass before I'd experience the PostNasal Gap again, but when I did, I'd be no less surprised than I'd been just now!

EIGHT

S afe in my amnesia, I checked my email again. There was an enthusiastic note from a filmmaker for whom I'd once done a script. He wanted to meet for lunch to talk about the possibility of "something funny but serious on picking." "If we can sharpen the parody," he wrote, "we've got something big." An editor I knew, from *New York Magazine*, wrote to alert me that I would soon hear from a writer to whom she'd assigned a piece on "punk blogs." Another message from Geek passed along data indicating that my blog was ranked 14th on Technorati.com, 49th on Chataction.com, and, amazingly enough, 45th on Radiotalk.com. I filed what needed to be filed and sent the rest to Carlotta, then turned to the most important of the messages I'd saved – a flattering response to my blog from Robert Fawck (**Figure 9**).

Fawck was not unknown to me. Like anyone who read the literary and science periodicals, I'd seen reviews of his books – the short one on Wittgenstein,[208] which had received a lot of attention, and the longer one on neurochemistry,[209] which

---

208 Fawck, Robert. *Notes on Wittgenstein* (Jackson, Mississippi: Philosophy Press, 1993).

209 **209** Fawck, Robert. *Neurochemistry on the Edge* (St. Louis, Missouri: Washington University Press, 1998).

Figure 9   Robert Fawck.

was said to be incomprehensible to anyone outside the field. From a recent *Scientific American* program on PBS,[210] I also knew a bit about his biography. Now forty-one, he'd published the first of his neuroscience papers ten years earlier, his first philosophy papers ten years before that. He was principally known for his so-called "normal dysfunction" theory, the idea that, as he'd explained on the PBS program, a healthy human brain is an oxymoron. "How can we call 'healthy' an organ which generates constant, chaotic, and brutally painful streams of thought, desire, and self-consciousness?"[211]

Nose-picking, he wrote, had long been a "useful and productive variable" in his work. "Brain-scan evidence shows us that the fundamental root of self-consciousness is a cluster of cells in the insula which is essentially deactivated during rhinotillexis. In effect, picking is liberation from

Figure 10   Denis Haggerty.

210   PBS. *Scientific American* July 19, 2008. See also *Scientific American Highlights* CD-ROM (PBS At-Home Video, 2003). And of course, Rfawck.com, where it remains available for viewing and/or download. See also *Robert Fawck: The Voice of Nasalism*, an essay collection edited by Alva Harrison, and *Nasalism, An Anthology* edited by David Crimmins, both of which contain transcripts of this program (New York: Murgate, 2012).

211   Fawck, *Neurochemistry on the Edge*, op. cit., 25. **Figure 9.**

self-consciousness. One doesn't watch himself while doing it. In the deepest sense, in fact, one is not even aware of doing it." Since he was, as he wrote, a "close to fanatic picker" himself, it was no surprise that he and Klondyke had begun to work together after the latter had moved from John Hopkins to MIT. In fact, as I'd soon learn when I visited their lab at MIT, the work for which they'd win the Lasker Award in 2012[212] was already completed.

Fawck did not mention this in his email. As in most of our correspondence, which was now to become a daily habit for both of us, he was personal, confidential, and, obviously, a wonderful source of scientific validation for the practice.

> "For a scientist whose subject is freedom from thought, who's been forced to search out such freedom in psychoactive drugs or sublime behavior like laughter and meditation, it's no small thing to come upon an ordinary act which neutralizes the insula. As an antidote for brain damage, only sex at the moment of orgasm rivals nose-picking."[213]

I scanned the MIT brochure and forwarded it to Sara and Geek, then sent it, with my first three blogs and the information I'd just received from Murgate's publicity office, to Peter Conrad, Carlotta, and the four researchers – Ann Curtis in Australia, Alan Fortas in New Zealand, Joe Johnson in Kansas City, and Phillip Baum in Birmingham, Alabama – who'd worked for me on *9/11* and *Terrorism*. Within an hour, I had enthusiastic replies from Phillip and Joe and by evening, when it was morning in Australia and New Zealand, I'd have the same from Ann and Alan.

Clicking onto Rhinotillexis.com again, I took advantage

212   Fawck, Robert and Klondyke, Marcus. "Images of Nasalism," *Science* April 2011: 46–55.

213   See Linchak, *The Complete Book of Nasalism*, op. cit., 248. Also, *Robert Fawck Letters*, edited by Alva Harrison (New York: Murgate, 2012).

of the new fiber-optic Internet connection, which Murgate had installed for me, to download – in less than a minute – Klondyke's book. Scanning it with excitement, I realized how far we'd come since those days, in the last decade of the 20th century, when the activity he researched was hardly acknowledged, much less investigated. Including websites as well as hard copy publications, his bibliography alone was an educational adventure. In addition to Denis Haggerty (**Figure 10**), for example, it directed me to Coribundi.com (**Figure 11**), which offered a videostream of "ritualized tillexis." Through the website of British sociologist Patricia Blake, I explored current research on "tillexic addiction"[214] and, by means of a sublink Blake provided, Colin Threlkeld's[215] attempt to treat that same addiction with group therapy based on the twelve-step Alcoholics Anonymous model.[216]

214   Blake, Patricia. *Compulsion and Addiction* (London: Oxford University Press, 2005).

215   Threlkeld, Colin. *Twelve Steps to Freedom* (Mexico City: Waking Dream Press, 2007). Also, "Twelve-Step Warrior," *New York Magazine* October 13, 2007.

216   See Antinasalism.com, 12stepdoctorate@Tulane.edu, Donewithpicking.com, Masteryourhabit.org, and for overview, Wikipedia, Twelve-Step Programs and Obsessive-Compulsive Disorder. Also, the AntiNasalism subsidiary of the online recovery community, ORC.com, and Serenity, the DVD collection of twelve-step workshops conducted monthly at Spiritual House, Darien, Connecticut.

Figure 11 Coribundi Indians, before entering their so-called "Igliesia Picotear" in Corcovado, Costa Rica, to commence the ritual they call "Extracto Santo." The ritual itself, as Haggerty and other anthropologists have reported, has never been photographed. Nathan Xaltur, second from right, was at the time of this photograph webmaster of Coribundi.com. Greatly influenced (as he notes in his blog) by his encounters with Haggerty, he was soon to emigrate to the United States and enroll at the University of Massachusetts. In 2011, he was awarded his PhD in Rhinology from MIT, where Klondyke was his thesis adviser. His doctoral thesis, "Sacred Nasalism," was published – with photographs by Haggerty – by Murgate in 2012 and Penguin in 2014. The first seven chapters of his anxiously awaited autobiography are currently available on his blog, Nathanxaltur162.com. He is now an Associate Professor at Ohio State. The man on his right is thought to be his uncle, Charlie Ray Xaltur, who replaced him as webmaster.

NINE

I n appreciation for my first blog, the webmaster of Coribundi.com sent me four ounces of high-quality Rhinobate. Needless to say, Sara and I quickly developed the habit of taking it together. Most evenings we did so after dinner and then, sitting across the table or sometimes in bed, waited in silence while it took effect. It was on one such evening, ten days after my first experience of the PostNasal Gap, that I encountered it once again.

By this time her practice was, if anything, more intense than my own. I was every day more astonished by the changes in her. The first thing she did every morning was click onto Ettingoff's website or blog. As she noted on her own blog, she was working hard to absorb Maggie's "deeper and more spacious view of the practice – that it's not simply a matter of extraction but the sincerity with which one pursues it. The ultimate goal is to pick without vanity, strip one's mind of ulterior motive so that picking is finally an end in itself."[217]

Fierce in her discipline, she soaked her fingertips twice a day in a solution of hydrogen peroxide and flaxseed oil, cleaned her nostrils every night with cotton swabs dipped in an herbal solution she'd ordered (because, like Rhinobate, it was used

---

217   Martinson, Sara. Saramartinson.com, March 18, 2011. See also, her memoir, op. cit., 23–34.

by the Coribundi) through Coribundi.com, and – following Ettingoff's advice – practiced what was called "ritualistic picking" every two hours, whether she had a crust or not.[218] Like me, she cataloged her significant crusts, photographing (with a state-of-the-art web-cam mounted on her monitor) those she considered unusual. Reading with her characteristic speed, she'd been through *Rhinotillexis* and *Among the Coribundi* and, determined to propagate the practice, contacted many of the writers Klondyke referenced with an eye to publishing them in the future.

Why was she so devoted? Mickey's view – offered to me in an email – was that it was all about sex. "Given that nose-picking is essentially a form of masturbation, how can we be surprised – especially when we're dealing with a woman so frigid – when it is eroticized?"[219] As often, I disagreed with his generalizations, but about Sara it was hard to argue with him. Easy access to orgasm is a gift to anyone, but for her, a woman for whom "coming," as she writes in the memoir, "is every time like climbing Mt. Everest,"[220] it seemed, as she had said to me more than once in the aftermath of sex, "a gift from God."[221]

Given such intensity, all the intimacy we owed to the practice, it's no small understatement to say that PostNasalism

---

218   Many who practice "ritualistic picking" agreed with the blogger who calls himself Constantpick.com that "picking which requires a crust to proceed is "profane" and "materialistic." Needless to say, there is considerable argument as to whether "ritualistic picking" is distinct from "idio-picking" but Constantpick [see his blog, June 3, 2008 as well as the recent Amazon/Kindle anthology of his blogs, *Constantblog* (Amazon.com) 134], as well as many of his correspondents, considers the distinction irrelevant. Perhaps we should not be surprised that there are those, even among his own correspondents, who call this view heretical, and of course, no small number of rhinopsychologists who call it "ignorant" or "naive." For an excellent summary of this still unresolved argument as well as a surprising portrait of Constantpick himself, see Alva Harrison, *A Brief History of Nasalism* (New York: Knopf) 233–276.

219   Linchak, Mickey. Mlinchak.com, February 18, 2011.

220   Martinson, op. cit., 48.

221   Ibid., 58.

was not part of our equation. Despite her every-two-hour ritual, she was as passionate about extraction as she was about sex and, for all her conviction, extremely dependent on my support. The last thing she needed was to see me hesitating, as I did that night.

Twelve minutes had passed since we'd inhaled, and the drug had produced its usual effects. As always with rhinobatoids, my crusts were bilateral and aggressive. The patience I felt with regard to them was as inexplicable and disorienting as it had been before.

Sitting across the kitchen table, wearing the orange hooded Murgate sweatshirt she wore almost every evening for these sessions, she was nursing a cup of green tea and an oatmeal raisin cookie which (picked up by her driver at a Midtown bakery both of us favored before he circled back and picked her up at the office) had also become a featured part of our ritual. Her extraction had been typically single-minded. Though concentrated, preoccupied, and actually somewhat troubled while she picked, her face was relaxed and blissful now as she enjoyed the experience she describes in the first chapter of her memoir as well as (identically) in the first of her nasal blogs: "The feeling that all desire is satisfied, that I haven't the slightest inclination to be anything other than what I am at that moment."[222] It was then she became aware that both my hands were motionless.

"Are you okay?"

"Yes. Why do you ask?"

"Wasn't your dose equal to mine?"

"Far as I know."

"Well, what's going on?"

"Why do you ask?"

Needless to say, as I've more than once acknowledged, I

---

222   Martinson, op. cit., 17.

was nowhere near the innocence I professed. In addition to the feelings I'd known before, I had now to deal with the not inconsiderable pressure of her expectation. If patience seemed a rejection of Nasalism, my inaction seemed a rejection of her.

As Partridge notes, however, (quoting me directly[223]) I'd always underestimated her and I was doing so now again. Though she had so far been spared the trauma of Post Extraction Despair, she was no novice anymore. In fact, she was well on her way to the Second Gate. Thanks to Ettingoff – whose ideal, frequently stated, was "process, not product,"[224] – she'd begun to explore a larger and not entirely negative view of the time between crusts or what Fawck likes to call the "nasal void."[225] Though unaware of it as yet, her practice – as her blog would acknowledge in retrospect – was becoming every day less goal oriented.[226] To her surprise as well as my own, she had more sympathy and tolerance for me than either of us could understand.

She finished her cookie with her left hand, wiped her right forefinger on the edge of the insulated glass container in which she stored her crusts, then leaned across the table and kissed me on the forehead. "Jesus," she sighed. "Forgive me, okay?"

"For what?"

"Challenge your fear and you challenge everything. Once you take this road, you can't know what to expect. All bets are off! Hardly a day goes by when I don't want to back off. Why should you be different?"

"I haven't backed off."

"No? What's happening then?"

---

223 Partridge, *Linchak, a Biography*, op. cit., 216

224 Ettingoff, Maggie. Mettingoff.com, August 12, 2009. See also, Ettingoff.com and "Ritualized Practice," *Extract* May 2011: 59–63.

225 Fawck, Robert. Rfawck.com, September 15, 2009 (among others).

226 Martinson, Sara. Saramartinson.com, March 21, 2011. "Movement away from goal-oriented, 'crust-centered' practice is the first step on the way to PostNasalism."

"I'm just… waiting."

"For what?"

"I don't know."

"You're not uncomfortable?"

"Sure I am."

"Both sides?"

"Yes."

"Congested?"

"Yes."

"So what's going on?"

"Nothing's going on. I'm just waiting."

She closed one eye. "Well maybe all bets are off, but one thing I know for sure is you'll always surprise me. Always have and always will. I've never understood you. Why on earth should I do so now?"

"Well, I surprise me too," I said. "I haven't a clue what's going on."

She shook her head and shrugged her shoulders. "Wow," she said. "That's beautiful. You did it again."

Figure 12 *Noseweek* cover, February 15, 2011. Even today, it is frequently seen on T-shirts, buttons, bumper-stickers, magnetic automobile ribbons, toilet paper, and of course facial tissue.

TEN

I t was two weeks later that President Bush appeared on "Larry King Live." At George's request, the producers asked me to appear with him, but, with Nasalism becoming every day more ubiquitous in the media and on the Internet, the last thing I wanted was to subject it to the inane chatter that talk shows, no matter how much I tried to contain myself, drew out of me. George, of course, shared none of my fears. Even now, in the aftermath of his depression, he was totally comfortable on TV. I have to say he made me proud, not just because he gave me credit for his recovery, but because he presented the practice unapologetically, with just enough imprudence to keep it free of respectability. Of course, there were those – J.J., for example, webmaster of Booger.com, and Harriet Pierce, whose Pickawinner.com is even more popular[227] today than it was then – who were furious about his appearance. The "Booger Blogs," as Lundy called them, would rail about it for days. I wasn't completely free of the fears they voiced, of course, but when the interview was over, there was no doubt in my mind that he'd helped us more than he'd hurt us. If I had any doubts about that, I had only to consult the famous *USA Today*/Gallup Poll, taken two days

---

[227] Not only popular, but lucrative, according to Internetadvertise.com, with more than a thousand hits a day, it attracts more advertising – for facial tissue and inhalers – than any other Nasalist website.

later, in which 91.2% admitted that the program had made them "respect" nose-picking and 67% expressed the hope that they'd one day be able to do it in public.[228]

Say this first: he was altogether free of the cheerleader style he'd maintained as a president. The only sign of his psychological instability was the fact that he wore the flight suit and carried the helmet he'd worn on the aircraft carrier when proclaiming "Mission Accomplished" in Iraq. About this, however, as about his practice, his candor made him more sympathetic than embarrassing. Soon after King introduced him, he explained that he wore the flight suit as often as possible these days because he wanted to remind his supporters as well as himself of the "courage" and "conviction" he'd lost in the last two years of his presidency. "Iraq did it. Losing Congress in '06 did it. Those were rough years, Larry. We forgot what it means to be Americans. I've been down ever since because I blame myself for it. It's only in the last few weeks that I've begun to see some light again. Nowadays, I'll do anything to keep that light alive, even if it means wearing a flight suit that most people think I should never a-worn in the first place."

In recent years, Bush's reputation had taken hits even worse than those he'd known while he was president, but if the ratings and polls were accurate, his appearance that night went a long way toward restoring it. According to a *New York Times*-CBS Poll the following day, 87% of the audience – which Neilsen estimated to have been bigger, by 12%, than the total audience for the last Super Bowl – found him "believable," 81% "appealing," and 80% "presidential."[229] Even now, it remains the most popular of all YouTube videos, and the DVD – which combined that evening's interview with the one that Oprah did in the clinic – continues to outsell almost anything else on the market.

---

228 *USA Today*/Gallup Poll. "Health and Well being," April 4, 2011.

229 *The New York Times*-CBS Poll. "Bush on Larry King," April 3, 2011.

I'd never been a fan of King's but I have to say he was impeccable that night. After a few minutes of pro-forma talk about mental illness and depression (interrupted by commercials for Prozac, a new sleep medication, and the American Institute of Depression) and a quick segue to dismiss ("unconvincingly," according to almost every blog or review I read) the rumor that George had attempted suicide the day after the 2006 elections and, again, the day before he and Laura moved out of the White House in 2009, King said, "Okay, Mr. President, I've got to ask the tough question: is it true what we hear about your recovery?[230] Do you really credit it to something most of us call a bad habit?"

George laughed. "Slow down, Larry! You're heading for trouble. You sure you want to talk about it?"

"No thanks, Mr. President. You wouldn't respect me if I backed off! Tell us everything!"

"Well, I don't call it a bad habit, Larry, but most people do. Laura does. My parents do. Karl Rove does. I haven't asked him, but I'd guess Dick Cheney does. If I agreed with them, I'd still be depressed, but thank God, I've found my way to a different point of view. That's why I'm out of the hospital."

"What's the habit we're talking about?"

George put his finger on the tip of his nose and kept it there as he spoke. "Some people call it 'nose-picking.' I call it plain, down-home taking care of business. Something bothers you, go after it! One moment you're uncomfortable, the next you're not! It's as simple as that, but Godamighty, it makes you feel good! Show me anyone on earth who doesn't know that!

---

230 King's reference, it should be noted, was a result of the widespread publicity which had followed the *Huffington Post* article by Nelson Brinstein: "Bush a Nose-Picker." Repeated first by the tabloids, then by hundreds of blogs and online magazines, then the serious press and news programs, the headline had made his habit such old news by now that it was rarely mentioned except as a tag-line for other pieces on the practice – editorials, interviews of his family, his supporters, members of his former cabinet, and "experts" (Klondyke, for example) on the psychology of the habit and the political implications of his admission.

Ninety-nine out of 100 people, no, make that 999 out of a 1,000, they do it two or three, hell, maybe twenty times a day, but how many admit it? How many do it in public or even in front of their family? No, most people are like me. Leastways like I used to be. Hide in the bathroom and don't admit it even to themselves! Most folks – they don't even like to look in the mirror! It's a simple habit, natural, basic – clean yourself, take care of yourself, get rid of what's bothering you – but its hidden behind a wall of pussyfoot hypocrisy!"

He'd been relatively calm until this moment but all of a sudden he was visibly agitated. Shifting in his chair, opening and closing his hands, he squinted at King as if a blinding light were shining in his eyes. An editorial in the next day's *Washington Post* called this moment, and what followed, a "public breakdown," and three months later, in the online edition of *The New England Journal of Medicine*, Harvard psychiatrist Marcia Thomas maintained that what came to the surface was "the inherent dry-drunk syndrome that made George W. Bush such a disaster as a president."[231] For me, or course, it was not a breakdown but a breakthrough. It was precisely for such an explosion that I'd been waiting – and hoping. Even those of us who've not yet passed the First Gate know that it is detachment more than anything else our insertions challenge. Picking is not an idea. It is *concrete reality*. The truth that dissolves illusion. This alone is what makes it so profound. Words may point at it but if you want to communicate what it's about, you've got to throw off ideas and words and… *just do it*. For Anti- or NonNasalists watching just then, George's agitation was shocking or even pathological, but anyone who's embarked on this Path understood at once that he was feeling the shame and anger we all feel when we dilute or intellectualize the practice in order to make it reasonable or tasteful, palatable to the other side.

231 Thomas, Marcia. "Bush's Syndrome," *The New England Journal of Medicine* July 2011: 87–90.

Grasping his flight helmet he stood and faced the camera, leaning across the table. "Can I have a close-up, please?"

Dutifully, the camera zoomed for the first of the famous frontal shots which, despite the fact that most newspapers except the tabloids[232] refused to print it, is said to be – by means of YouTube and other Internet distribution – the most widely viewed of any photograph in history.[233] On my email the following day alone, I received more than sixty messages to which this image was attached, and I'm sure I emailed at least that many myself.

He stared into the camera for a moment, then slowly inserted his right forefinger. Unconstrained by timidity or embarrassment, his finger turned, probed, turned again, pulled back slightly, probed again. When finally he spoke, he did not withdraw. "How many times has this been seen on TV? Once? Twice? Never? What does it say about our country or, for that matter, the whole world that something we all do – every day! More than once! – can't be shown by the media? Why should we hide it? What's to be ashamed of? I didn't know this until a great friend of mine, a great American – Walker Linchak – made me wake up, face the music, give up my lies once and for all!"

One watched in astonished disbelief as his finger continued its exploration, but when finally he withdrew, a greater surprise awaited us. Dangling from his finger was at least a 7, possibly an 8. Surely, Crimmins does not exaggerate when he calls it "the most significant crust in history."[234] Even the most advanced Nasalists questioned its arrival at a moment so auspicious. Many believed it artificial, a product of makeup technicians or special effects, but later, in an email to me, George himself would agree

---

232   Among them, *The New York Post* April 3, 2011, under the headline: "PICK OF THE PRESIDENTS."

233   Digitalview.com, June 1, 2013.

234   Crimmins, David. "Bush's Breakthrough," *Rhinology Alert* August 2011: 19–23.

with Fawck[235] that it was simply fortuitous, produced by the situation itself. In effect, his yearning for, and faith in crusts had, as he put it, "generated a state of inspiration that focused in my nose."[236]

Needless to say, coagulation began at once. Continuing now, he held it suspended, angled slightly in King's direction. "But I'll tell you something, Larry – I wouldn't have understood Linchak if it hadn't been for my depression. When you're down like I was, looking for help wherever you can, the truth is your friend! I read that blog… and damn it, I understood! Said to myself, 'Man, you been hiding! You do it and pretend you don't! Not only that – you love it! It clears your nose and it clears your mind and while you do it, you damn well don't do anything else!' Look a-here, Larry – this thing in your nose… it's attacking you! What's more natural than fighting back? What feels better? Tell me anything dumber than being ashamed of it! Once I admitted this to myself, I felt a hundred times better. Depression was over and done with! I'm gonna stay in the clinic for another week but I tell you for sure, I'm done with depression! I'm a healthy man again!"

He stretched his hand toward the camera, extending the finger he'd inserted. "No, it aint a bad habit, Larry. The bad habit is lying to yourself! Being a good boy! You think dishonesty don't hurt you, tell yourself it's no big deal, but then depression hits, and you know it's been eating you up inside! You can't get up in the morning. You've got no energy, no enthusiasm, no feeling. Worst of all, the lie has spread through your life! Aint a shred of honesty in you! I been there, Larry! But I aint going back!"

If the show had ended there, it would still have been, for

---

235 Fawck, Robert. Rfawck.com, April 12, 2011.

236 Cavanaugh, *Bush and Linchak*, op. cit., 34. See also, the recently issued collection of our correspondence. *Bush-Linchak, A Friendship*, edited by Nehmiah Robbins (Sewanee, Tennesse: Sewanee Press, 2013).

those already on the Path as well as the thousands who, thanks to George, would now be inspired to join us, cause for celebration, but after a long pause (the longest ever seen, according to one reviewer, on "Larry King Live"), King himself took it further. "I know that many will be shocked by what you've said, Mr. President, but I'm not one of them. I'll say it right here on the air: I practice this habit myself. I do it often and I don't mind saying I enjoy it. But I'm no more honest about it than you were! I never do it in public! Even my wife and kids have never seen me do it. You've done us all a great service, sir. I've always admired your courage but you've never shown it more than you have tonight."

As we know, the close-up images from the interview have remained immensely popular through the years, but even more popular – as a YouTube, Google, and Yahoo image and also as a poster – is the parody of a *Newsweek* cover which appeared four days later under the title *Noseweek* (**Figure 12**). Showing George, flight helmet under his arm, standing proudly with crust extended toward King under a banner reading "Mission Accomplished,"[237] it was said to be the work of a group of renegade *Newsweek* employees who, according to most reports,[238] were angry that *Newsweek* editors, believing it too controversial, had killed the same cover in-house just hours before it was scheduled for print. Whatever its source, it's safe to say that no magazine cover has been more often reproduced. Some believe that the controversy it generated was greater than that produced by the interview itself. Most of the commentary, like an editorial in *The New York Times*[239] and that which was voiced on "Meet the Press" the following

237 *Noseweek*, April 6, 2011. **Figure 12.**

238 *The New York Times*, April 11, 2011.

239 *The New York Times*, April 8, 2011; "Meet the Press" (Condoleeza Rice, Colin Powell, Rudolph Giuliani), April 13, 2011.

week, took it for granted that George as well as the Republican Party were humiliated by the cover, but George himself had a different take on it. In his next TV appearance, an interview with Bill Moyers on PBS, he expressed nothing but pride in it. Indeed, the original *Noseweek* print is said to hang in his office to this day. "What's wrong with that cover? I'll take it any day! I accomplished more in that interview than I did as a president and I'm happy to see it appreciated!"

ELEVEN

On the morning after the interview, Peter Conrad received sixteen proposals for a book and seven for a magazine piece about my relationship with George, as well as more than fifty requests (newspapers, radio and television shows, online and print magazines, etc.) for interviews. Quoting often from *Bush and Linchak*, the media, of course, covered the interview extensively, and for weeks it remained, according to most surveys, the dominant subject in the blogosphere. As for George and Nasalism, my first inkling of what would soon become a groundswell was an email from a graduate student named Jane O'Hara at UCLA's Department of Media Studies who had obtained my address from my blog. She attached a brief synopsis of her PhD dissertation on "Media and Privacy." Since the Bush interview, she said, had brought "public awareness" to "a private habit," it was obviously relevant to her thesis. "I'd appreciate your exchanging emails on this issue and I'd be most grateful if you'd give me Mr. Bush's email address so that I can discuss it with him."

Another email came from Fawck:

"I'm thinking more and more about Third Gate amnesia. I'd not disagree with those who relate it to the neurological trauma of the PostNasal Gap, but I'd like to reverse the equation and investigate the effect of patience on the brain. In any event, there's one thing I'm certain of – nothing so much as PostNasalism demonstrates the absurdity of separating psychology and neurology."[240]

Despite the fact that I would eventually come to agree with him (indeed, to write an article in support of his views for *Brain Mind Digest*[241]), I was still too much bewildered by patience to consider it rationally. Even more bewildering was the fact that, like many who've known the PostNasal Gap, I was experiencing the "Nasal Fecundity"[242] which, depending on whether you lean toward Fawck or Klondyke, is either a "happy byproduct of patience"[243] or a symptom of "PostNasal anxiety."[244] My crusts appeared with unusual frequency, and extractions produced extreme, or what Stanford rhinopsychologist, Herman Haggar, calls "hysterical,"[245] satisfaction. More disconcerting still was my behavior at those times ("our lacuna," Maggie calls them[246]) when I had no crusts at all. Again and again, I found myself engaged in what Haggar calls "idiopathic tillexis,"[247] or Fawck, "idio-picking."[248] In effect, I picked for no reason. It was

---

240   I was soon to discover, via the next issue of *Science Times*, that the work of which he spoke was already well advanced, its progress sadly accelerated by the death of his dear uncle, Jeremy Fawck, whom his nephew considered "the most courageous practitioner I've ever known. **Figure 13.**

241   Linchak, Walker. "The Neurology of Patience," *Brain Mind Digest* August 2011: 77–81.

242   Fawck, *Nasal Metaphysics*, op. cit., 211.

243   Ibid.

244   Klondyke, Marcus. "Tillexophobia," *Extract* August 2011: 23–98.

245   Haggar, Herman. Stanfordrhinology.edu.

246   Ettingoff, *Nasalism My Way*, op. cit., 212–215.

247   Haggar, op. cit.

248   Fawck, *NeoNasalism*, op. cit., 23–38.

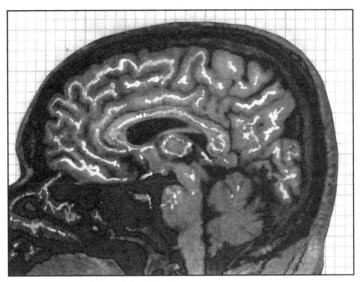

Figure 13 *Autopsied brain of Jeremy Fawck.*
    Fawck's first article on Post Nasalism featured the above autopsied brain of his uncle, Jeremy Fawck. According to his memoir, *Patience All the Way* (New York: Murgate, 2014), the elder Fawck converted to PostNasalism in June 2012 and "never looked back." He died (of cardiac arrest) at the age of 78, one month before his memoir was published, in April 2014. His oversized insula and remarkably thin neocortex – "inarguable confirmation," wrote Fawck, "of the effect of patience on the tissue in which it occurs" – were first noted by pathologist, Carrie Mast, who conducted the autopsy.

as if the act had become autonomous and self-fulfilling or, internalizing Ettingoff's warnings about goal-oriented practice, I had completely lost touch with its motivation. The result was that my finger was more often in my nose than not. Sara, of course, was proud of me for this. As far as she was concerned, my perseveration was practice, discipline, another reason to reprimand herself for mistrusting my hesitation. Needless to say, I found no comfort in her pride. I was more and more disturbed by my behavior. As luck would have it, however, the email from Fawck was followed by several from my staff that, by amazing coincidence, included information on "waiting" and "patience" and even idio-picking itself. Ann Curtis forwarded an article by Haggar which had appeared two years earlier in the *Journal of Rhinology*, and Joe Johnson, using LexisNexis, had found a wonderful piece by Haggerty, of all people, on "obsessive-compulsion in the Coribundi." I'd always been able to count on my staff for this sort of help, but with *The Complete Book of Nasalism*, I'd see time and again how much I'd underestimated them. Within a week, both Ann and Joe would find their way to research (Colin Threlkeld's, of course, among others) that related idio-picking to "rhinotillexic addiction" as well as abrasion and, even worse, infection, and Alan Fortas would forward the website of Nelson Goldstein, at Hadassah Hospital, in Jerusalem, where I'd find data which connected idio-picking to pulmonary fibrosis and/or, like fibrosis itself, auto-immune disease.[249] I should mention too that Constantpick's blog claimed to represent a group built around "endless" and "self-contained" picking which, as one of its correspondents stated, "is its own reward. Indeed, those who focus on extraction are nothing but gross materialists." One could not discern how many belonged to this group, but according to Technorati.com, the site averaged more than a hundred hits a day over the three-year period, 2006–2009.

---

[249] Goldstein, Nelson. "Auto-immune Compulsion," *International Pulmonology* Vol. 211 (August 2011) 233–246. It should be noted that Goldstein's work had already evoked argument from researchers who related idio-picking – as eventually they'd relate Nasalism itself – to a virus.

TWELVE

I t was from George himself, by way of an email five days later, that I first heard of his vlog. Until then, he'd been fairly naïve about computer technology, but his friendship with Geek Williams brought him up to date.[250] As I've mentioned, Geek had helped him, some said criminally, in both national elections, and they'd remained in contact by email and phone ever since. Were it not for their friendship, I suspect that George might never have heard of bloging, much less vlogging, but when he talked with Geek after the Larry King interview, he said he wanted his own blog. "I want to continue what I started the other night. I need to speak to the people every day. Why should I wait for the TV honchos to give me permission? I want to speak from my own room with nobody looking over my shoulder." Geek replied, "Why not go all the way?" George had no idea what he meant, but a few minutes later, a vloging program, with precise directions for installation and set-up, was in his email box.

Next day, booting up, I found he'd emailed his new address. "Take a look at the new me. You've no one but yourself to blame."

---

250 Wikipedia.com. "Vlogs also often take advantage of video-stream technology to allow for the distribution of video over the Internet using either the RSS format or syndication formats, for automatic aggregation and playback on mobile devices and personal computers. Though many vlogs are collaborative efforts, the majority of vlogs and vlog entries are authored by individuals."

One click later, his face was on my screen. Once again, he was wearing his flight suit. The crash helmet he'd cradled on the carrier sat on the desk in front of him. My heart sunk when I saw this, but he put me at ease immediately. "Take a look, my friends. Have you ever seen anything more ridiculous than me in this outfit?"

He paused and turned his back to the camera, facing the mirror behind him. A moment later, when he turned around, his words were halting and his eyes downcast. "A kid dressed up for Halloween. That's what I was as a president. Trick or treat, America! Take a look! This is the man you elected. A man who had as much business being president as he had doing brain surgery or pitching for the Astros. Who brought you Iraq and tax cuts for the rich and contempt for the environment and totally stupid, cruel indifference after Hurricane Katrina. Remember him standing on the deck of the carrier with the banner spread out behind him? 'Mission Accomplished?' How many died after that? How many billions of dollars down the drain? Take a look, America! Here's the guy who shit on the Constitution! Made a mockery of the White House! Trick or treat! The time for lies is over!"

Response to his outburst was predictably adversarial. And superficial. At one end of the spectrum were those who considered it sick and delusional or, as Dick Cheney said a few days later on "Meet the Press," "political suicide." At the other were those, like me and other Nasalists, who saw it as an epiphany, a "rhino-transformation" of the sort we'd all experienced. Neurologically speaking, both sides, of course, were, naïve. If we'd had access to the brain-scan work which was already in progress at MIT, we'd have realized that the George W. Bush who spoke to us on the vlog was a totally different human being from the one we'd known as president or, in my case, as a friend. More surprise, of course, was in store for us. We'd just begun to see the real effects of his transformation. Even those of us who'd experienced the practice underestimated the degree to which – by altering his neurochemistry, changing the relationship between his limbic brain and his cerebral cortex – Nasalism had healed the brain damage which had crippled George throughout his life.

The flight suit was gone in the following day's vlog, replaced by a T-shirt and jeans which made him look as young and athletic as in the early days of his presidency. Even so, he was still preoccupied with his appearance on the carrier. "Most of my enemies think I was out-and-out lying when I spoke from the carrier, but I'll tell you what's really nuts. I believed every word I said! I thought we'd won the fucking war! Why not? A few months before, I thought Saddam had weapons of mass destruction! Why is that? How is it possible that a man with access to the best intelligence in the world can be such a stupid fucking idiot? They told me Saddam aint nothing we need to worry about. Told me we'd have a civil war on our hands. Jesus, they told me we were doing exactly what the terrorists wanted us to do! So why did I do it? Why was I standing on the goddamn carrier like king of the fucking world? Because I was a man who believed what he wanted to believe, that's why! Saw what he wanted to see! All my life I'd been that way! Living in a dream! That's the guy you elected, my friends! THE GUY YOU RE-ELECTED! Your Fuck-up-in-Chief. Take a look! You wanted lies and you got them!"

He took a step back from the camera, closed his eyes for a moment and took a deep breath. "But I'm gonna say it again, my friends. Those days are over!" He put his finger on the tip of his nose. "Like they say, it don't matter how long your trip is. You got to begin with your first step. Well, this is mine! Right now, here, watch me, goddamn it! I'm not anymore a liar. I put my finger here, I know what it means to tell the truth. Resist, hold back, hide out in the bathroom, I know what it cost me, all these years, to live a life of bullshit."

THIRTEEN

I n late April, four months after I'd set out on the Path, a weekend of meetings launched the campaign *The New York Post* announced with a mean-spirited Page Six headline "PICKAWINNER."[251] Andre Mannheim, in his *Murgate: A History*, calls it "the most effective media blitz the world has ever seen."[252] The first meeting was called for 9 a.m. on a Friday morning in the conference room on the 58th floor. It was a huge room with high ceilings, thick wall-to-wall carpet, set up today with rows of leather chairs. We were filmed as we came off the elevators by Luisa Maxoni, a documentary filmmaker whose last two features[253] had been produced by Murgate subsidiary, Vox3 Films. She'd set up with a sound-man, two cameramen, a gaffer, a grip, and a handheld camcorder she operated herself. The footage she collected that day would become the opening of the PBS documentary. She'd already interviewed George and me and Sara and Geek, of course, and she was soon to connect with others, like Fawck and Klondyke, who figured significantly in the movement.

It was proof of the meeting's importance that almost everyone was less than half an hour late. One by one, we took our seats and ordered food and drinks from circulating waiters.

---

251   *The New York Post*, April 29, 2011.

252   Mannheim, Andre. *Murgate: A History* (New York: Norton, 2011).

253   Maxoni, Luisa. Director, *Earth Times* (2006) and *Edge of Yonder* (2009).

George was there, of course, arriving with Larry King just a few minutes after Sara and me. Even at a distance, I was struck by his reticence and serenity. Nodding toward us, he took a seat in the front row and did not look around. Klondyke, Ettingoff, and Fawck arrived a moment after he did, taking seats in the row behind him. The rest of the crowd was distinguished: Howard Unterecker, Murgate's CEO; the CEOs of other Murgate companies like Microsoft, YouTube, Omega Institute, *Yoga Journal*, and *Tricycle*; various people from the art, public relations, and publicity departments of the parent company or its subsidiaries, etc.; and finally, the usual array of movie stars and athletes: Martin Scorsese and Brian DePalma, both of whom were doing films which Murgate's Lions Gate would distribute; Nicole Kidman, who was starring in the Scorsese film; Robert Downey, Jr., who was starring in the DePalma; Conway Hoover, the point guard recently drafted by Murgate's New York Knicks, etc. Celebrities weren't uncommon at meetings like this, of course, but in this case, they weren't here for decoration. Sara and Geek had plans for them. In fact, as we were soon to see, she'd already signed Kidman for the ad poster which, more than any other, would define the campaign and, as Unterecker put it, "legitimize the product."

I'd never doubted Sara, but after this meeting I had to admit I'd underestimated her in the extreme. She'd long been recognized as an editor, acquiring books and moving them down the line as well as anyone in publishing, but according to Mannheim, this campaign would establish her as a "promotional genius, an artist whose canvas was international media."[254] He quoted Unterecker: "In my view, no one had understood and exploited the true reach and power of a 21st century media conglomerate until this campaign unfolded. She was the first to orchestrate cooperation between our companies and, by doing

254 Mannheim, *Murgate: A History*, op. cit., 46.

so, the first to mobilize and utilize the arsenal we'd acquired."[255]

Introducing herself and welcoming everyone, she sat at a desk in the back of the room, the usual array of technology spread out before her: two computers, two monitors, wireless mice and keyboards, a bank of phones, and a console with flashing lights and countless buttons that looked like a fairly serious synthesizer. Booting up, she pressed buttons on the console to close the draperies and dim the lights. "I suspect there's no one in the room who hasn't seen this, but I don't think any of us would mind seeing it again." Activating the DVD from her computer, she played the Bush-King interview on the movie-size screen built into the wall at the front of the room. She did not bring up the lights when it was over. After we saw the two men stand and shake hands across the table, she said, "I can't imagine anything more presumptuous than adding my words to those we've heard from the President and Mr. King. I do have plenty to say however about the campaign we're launching this morning."

In the silence, we heard a run of rapid-fire clicks from her keyboard. "I hope you've all studied the package we emailed earlier this week. In any event, you know why we're here today." On the screen, we saw the image – developed by her and Geek in conjunction with the art department – which would dominate the campaign. Accompanied by a soundtrack that reminded me of Phillip Glass – because, as it turned out, Glass himself (a major Murgate property since its purchase of Harmony.com and its online music library) had written it – an animated finger at the bottom of the screen moved slowly toward an animated nose at the top. As they met, the image dissolved into the montage we'd see throughout the campaign in the commercials and ads, on TV and the Internet, and in the whole range of print media: an airline pilot picked in the cockpit; Hoover,

---

255 Ibid., 47.

the New York Knick, paused before shooting to pick at the free-throw line; a short-order cook picked above a griddle full with bacon and eggs; and finally, Kidman, dressed down and sexy in jeans and a tank top, picked before the mirror at her dressing table. Later, *Variety* would reveal that Murgate had paid her $12 million for this spot, but of course, as it turned out, the company got itself a bargain in the deal. Relaxed, informal, and completely unembarrassed, Kidman gave the act dignity and beauty while conveying its privacy, its ordinariness, and, closing her eyes as if in a trance at the moment of extraction, its supervening pleasure. Many said it was this spot, more than any other, that transformed the "habit" into a "practice" which was not just acceptable but cool, even glamorous. But of course there were other contenders when it came to this accolade – Hoover had already signed a contract which obligated him to pick in an actual game, and both Scorsese and DePalma were contracted to include images of picking in their next films.

Sara continued in the darkness. "None of us, I'm sure, underestimates the task we face today. We're a mass-market company dealing with a huge audience we need to grow every year for our shareholders. We're completely at the mercy of the ratings, risking our capital and reputation on the choices we make. Even with the president of the United States on our team, we're looking at steep odds against us. Such odds, however, don't intimidate us in the least. They are our inspiration, a perfect confirmation of the choice we've made. Our competitors fear taking risks. This is why most of them are dinosaurs. Paralyzed by their size, forced to play it safe and cater to audience expectation, they're stuck with an audience that's fragile and promiscuous. We play by different rules. Risk is our mandate! We didn't get where we are by being cautious and predictable. We got here by challenging our audience, taking it where it least expects to go, and in our view, the product that brings us here today will accomplish this as no other has before. As the

President said in the interview you saw just now, most people think of it as a bad habit. They find it hard to mention, much less pursue in public. This despite the fact that, when they're alone, they practice it frequently, with pleasure and concentration. What we aim to do is help them realize that they're not alone when they do it. They're a community! However much they differ in race, class, or nationality, education, life-style, income, or politics, they share this wonderful practice.

"In addition to President Bush, Nicole Kidman, and Conway Hoover, our campaign will present testimony from Hillary Clinton, Michael Jordan, Jesse Jackson, and John Updike that they are every one a picker. How can we doubt that millions will be inspired by their example? In a very short time, the taboo that surrounds this habit will be a distant, laughable memory! The world is diverse, a chaos of conflict and disagreement, but, in this secret, forbidden practice, we're all more alike than different. In other words, it is not nose-picking we'll promote. It's community! Democracy!

"Within a year, we'll publish a book by our most esteemed author, Walker Linchak, author of *The Complete Book of AIDS*, *The Complete Book of 9/11*, and *The Complete Book of Terrorism*. His new book will not only celebrate this habit but explore its history and the great mass of scientific research which justifies its value and its universality. After Linchak will come other books by respected authors who've researched and studied the practice. We're negotiating with philosophers, neuroscientists, anthropologists, and psychologists. Within months we'll see the public's perception of this habit completely transformed. Never again will it be underestimated, much less forbidden. Linchak's book will generate more controversy and therefore, we believe, more income than any we've published. We'll circulate and ventilate such controversy on our talk shows, our websites, our chat rooms, and our search engines, our magazines, our radio and TV stations, our newspapers. Finally, each of our subsidiaries will promote and disseminate the fact that it's not just pleasure we're selling. It's *personal freedom*! Freedom to follow your instincts! Freedom from inhibition! Freedom from repression and constraint and most important, freedom from the isolation to which we've all been condemned by the subterfuge and hypocrisy which have surrounded this simple, cleansing habit!

"Our preliminary studies indicate that less than 12% of Americans acknowledge practicing this habit, much less enjoying it. It's our bet, however, that within a year or even less perhaps, non-pickers will be rare, objects of sympathy, if not derision. The embarrassment and inhibition which surrounds the practice will come to be viewed as repressive and reactionary. Most important, our audience will see that it is not a group of isolated individuals but as I say… a community! We're all connected by this habit! As the President said to Larry King, we are all alike – exactly alike! – in the happiness it gives us! Tell me a more important mandate for an entertainment company than making its viewers aware of their connection to each other!

"But why, you ask, do we choose this habit? Let's be honest about it. First of all, because it's tasteless. Even a presidential endorsement can't erase that. But for an audience like ours, tasteless is a positive. Our viewers are sick of good taste and predictability. Every day they overdose on banal, overcautious entertainment and distraction. Bad taste is not an obstacle for them. It's the wake-up call for which they yearn, every time, when they turn on their TV, pick up a newspaper, or surf the Internet. Furthermore, it has two characteristics which anyone in media knows to be crucial – *it is both repressed and universal.* By bringing it out in the open, we'll make the private public and, as I've said, unite our viewers, free them from inhibition, help them feel more comfortable with themselves and more connected to each other.

"But of course the habit has individual as well as social

attributes. All of us know that it relieves anxiety and diverts the mind. You saw the President's interview! How better to show the benefits of this practice than its wondrous healing effect on his depression? Research explains this power! Scientists at MIT have shown that the act produces an immediate increase in endorphins! The effect on serotonin uptake receptors is even greater than that produced by antidepressants like Prozac and Zoloft! The DVD you'll receive this week will detail research showing that this practice promotes concentration, reduces stress, enhances optimism and self-confidence. There are indications of pulmonary and digestive benefits as well! Cures of alcoholism and drug addiction are everywhere in the literature! Is it any wonder one turns to it when agitated or depressed? If it can work a miracle for the president of the United States, think what it does for you and me and the rest of our audience!"

The lights came on and we took a short break. There were a number of people I wanted to talk to, of course, but I slipped away and headed for the bathroom. To say that my mind was not where I wished it to be is a gross understatement. I was minutes into a significant crust and, once again, not anxious to extract. Furthermore, unlike other times, I had no amnesia to protect me. I could not pretend that patience was unfamiliar to me. Which is not to say that I was without conflict. Waves of anxiety were balanced, almost exactly, by waves of equanimity in my mind. As Fawck would say, my patience was proof that I'd arrived at the Third Gate, my conflict proof that I'd not yet closed it behind me. Many have described the terror one feels at this moment, but it's hard to believe that anyone has known it as painfully as I knew it just then. After all, I was hardly a bystander in the campaign we were launching. I was the reason we'd all come together that day. Even though I finally extracted (a moderate crust, not at all interesting, something between a 6 and a 7, I'd guess), I returned to the conference room with a haunting sense of disloyalty.

Once we'd settled into our seats again, Unterecker took over the meeting. He was small and rotund, with a thick head of white hair, a full white beard, and a habit of gesticulating wildly and inappropriately when he spoke, flicking his hands left or right or raising a single, extended finger toward the ceiling. He'd been CEO at General Electric before coming over to Murgate and, before GE, at Boeing Aircraft. With each move he'd garnered so many millions in severance pay and sweetheart offerings that he was currently being sued by shareholders at all three companies. According to a recent New Yorker profile, he was worth two billion dollars. If you've read that profile or Mannheim's book or, for that matter, *The Complete Book of Nasalism*, you know the steps he outlined now. Indeed, since both Lewis and I quote Mannheim, who quotes from the tape Maxoni's team recorded that morning, all three books include verbatim the statement he delivered now.

After welcoming George, me, and every celebrity in the room, Unterecker began by acknowledging the skepticism, "even horror," with which he responded when Sara first presented the idea of our campaign to him. "I don't deny I'm a picker myself, but I'm also a businessman. Loss was all I saw when I looked at this proposal, no upside at all. But at Sara's insistence, I read the Linchak blogs, and they led me to the literature and research on this practice. The more I read, the more I wanted to know, and the more I realized that my original take had been, at best, intemperate. I thought, 'If this can happen for me, it can happen for our audience!' I wasn't entirely convinced but I was beginning to waver. Then I saw the President on "Larry King Live" and I was completely hooked. Next morning I woke up thinking that we'd be out of our minds to pass this up.

"But as any businessman knows, idea and execution are two different animals. We know where we're going, but how do we get there? The one thing we have to avoid is media bombast.

We're not after novelty here. With a taboo like this, we want the front door, not the back. No marginal figures in our advertising, only the most prestigious names. Ground the excitement – see what I mean? – before it takes off. No screaming, no hysteria, no self-congratulation, and please, no prime-time outrageous. Turn yourself into a freak show, you get the teenagers, maybe the twenty-somethings, but anyone older laughs you off. We're looking for all ages here, to hell with the generation gap. What we need above all is credibility, and we've got the means to get it. Every year, the Murgate Foundation gives away more than $700 million. We've never looked to coordinate funding with product, but why not? We support research into parapsychology at Duke, homeopathy at Tulane, UFOs at Texas A&M, alien abduction at Harvard. Why not nose-picking? Why not nasal secretion, nasal anatomy, nasal, for that matter, anything? It's not as if we're starting from scratch. The research is already happening! All over the world! George Willmark, at the University of North Dakota, has data showing reduction in systolic and diastolic blood pressures. Karin Lundstrom in Stockholm has shown improvement in sleep and relaxation variables. Why can't we back these people? Once you do, you get the science section of the *Times*! And once you get the *Times*, you get "Nova," Oprah, who knows, maybe Terry Gross! Research means argument and argument means talk and chat and op-ed, letters to the editor. We'll be up to our ears in controversy! There's a psychologist at NYU – Nathan Hammerstein – who calls the habit, what is it, 'a species of schizophrenia.' Infantilism, masturbation – look them up on the web! What do you get? Every time, a link to nose-picking! Give me argument and you give me ratings! I want mothers whose kids won't stop, dermatologists who treat sores in the nose, right-wingers who call it – forgive me, Mr. Pesident – Liberal, un-American. Let's hear from the fundamentalists on it! The Muslims and the skinheads! The rabbis, the priests, the PTA! We're looking at fights big-time, rage on all sides! There's no end to this! Once it starts, we won't be able to stop it! A year from now, we won't be worried about being taboo but about becoming a cliché."

After another break, we heard from various department-heads who fleshed out the campaign. Advertising projected another series of ads, using others beside Kidman. Finally, Geek took the mic to describe his "viral chat" software, explaining – as he'd explained to Sara and me just a few weeks before – how he was now able to "seed" chat room conversation, mail-lists, and the blogosphere with what he called "digital gossip."[256] "First we create the opinion, then we argue it. We can keep it going as long as we want." Geek had also developed talk-radio plans, cultivated thousands of callers, in India, Thailand, and the Philippines, who (with perfect American accents, developed by means of Microsoft's new "accent software") phoned into radio and TV talk shows. "No ad equals what you get from chat and talk-radio. Once established, the conversation feeds off itself, and once it's going, we activate our websites and our Internet polling software, publish numbers and demographics every day. Once you've got the polls, you've got the media. Magazines and newspapers and TV news. They'll pick up our numbers and move them along and improve them as they do so."

256   As we know from Geek's memoirs, published two years later by Murgate [*Geek's Prorgress* (New York: Murgate, 2013)], his software had been used by the Republican Party in the elections of 2000, 2004, and 2008.

FOURTEEN

After the meeting, Sara and I had dinner with George in the Penthouse. The restaurant was full but she had reserved the beautiful corner table where she and I had lunched together. Heads turned when we walked in, of course, but, taking a seat with his back to the window, George seemed not to notice them. It was almost as if he'd lost every trace of his public identity.

Spread out like a carpet below us, the city was a lattice of jewels interspersed with the red and green of traffic lights, the yellow lights of cars, and another jewel, a new-moon sliver that sat just above his right shoulder.

George was voluble and friendly but oddly anxious and distracted. His mood seemed forced. I thought his agitation might be related to the meeting, but such a view was another misconception of which the MIT research would disabuse me. Agitation is a constant for anyone who endures the sort of changes he was going through. In addition to the explosive honesty he was experiencing as a result of his practice, he was, as I was soon to discover, encountering PED for the first time.

Sara, of course, was in a state of exhilaration. Never more than a minimal drinker, she drank three cups of saki within minutes of sitting down and then ordered a beer from the waiter. Talking fast and shaking her head repeatedly, she said she couldn't believe what she'd been through that day. Even though they weren't entirely new to her, she said the "insights" about Nasalism and democracy had "exploded" during the meeting. "For weeks I've thought about the opportunity we have, but I didn't realize how deep this goes, how far it reaches, the amazing scope of its implications. We're gonna be the first media company to transform its audience into a community! We know what this means on an individual level but when you use the tools that we've acquired to crystallize and propagate it, you're talking global transformation!"

It's not generally known, but it was during that dinner, seven years ago, that she first mentioned the idea of nominating me for the Templeton Prize, which was awarded every year by the John Templeton Foundation for "Progress Toward Research or Discoveries about Spiritual Realities." The idea had occurred to her, she said, when she was about halfway through her introductory talk. She'd almost mentioned it then but, fearing her own "idealism," decided to let it percolate before she went public. Now it seemed a "no-brainer" to her. It was clear that I deserved the award or, more exactly, that it deserved me. She took my hand and stared into my eyes. "Think how much it will validate what we began today! We're not talking product or profit, entertainment or escape. If God is about connection, and we are helping our audience connect with each other, we're talking meaning and happiness, fundamental truth, the essence of religion! Every crust is a religious epiphany. You showed us that! You gave us that permission! Before you defined the Path, it was nothing but a forbidden habit. Imagine! Religious epiphany is taboo! You've liberated thousands from this ignorance! This is a gift to all mankind. If it's not religious, the word *religious* has no meaning! What do you think, George?"

"Like you said, it's a no-brainer."

"And by the way," she said, "Murgate makes six-figure grants to the Templeton Foundation every year. We can't control who wins, of course, but you better believe they'll listen to us when it comes to nominations."

George sipped his saki thoughtfully. "Why not go farther?" he said. "Religious activity is tax-exempt. Set up a foundation to cover the campaign. Get yourself a tax exemption. Once you do, you can write off everything. It's true you'll have to roll your profits into research and development, but you can write them off against the rest of your profit. I didn't go to Harvard Business School for nothing! Your salary, Walker's advance... like everything else, you can write 'em off! As far as the IRS is concerned, you're non-profit all the way! Even this meal is deductible!"

He dug into his pocket, took out his cell phone, and scrolled 'til he found what he wanted. "Call this guy Monday morning," he said. "Herman Rausch. Director of the IRS. One of the few appointments I made who's still around. For that matter, one of the few people in Washington who still returns my calls. Tell him I gave you his number. You'll have your exemption within a couple of weeks." He pressed some more buttons, scrolled again, pressed another button, closed his phone, and put it back in his pocket. "I just emailed his number to you. Don't be shy about using it."

FIFTEEN

I t was three days later that the most shocking of all the vlogs came online. Forgive me for quoting it here. I know that there are few people in the world who haven't seen it, but I ask you to imagine how I felt that day, sitting at my desk, seeing my old friend attack the practice which had changed my life.

"My fellow Americans, I have something very difficult to share with you today. As many of you know, I recently confessed to a lifelong habit of nose-picking. I said I wasn't ashamed of it, but I'm here to tell you that this was untrue. I was not being honest with you. Truth is, I wasn't being honest with myself. God knows I was often dishonest when I was president, but I'm sad to say I never said anything more dishonest than I did that day."

Closing his eyes, he placed his left forefinger on the tip of his nose and, in the gesture we'd seen so often when he was president, his right hand on his chest. "Never once did I put my finger up here without hating myself for doing it! Never once! I don't care what names you give it, what fancy ideas you wrap it in, it's a terrible, stupid habit! I was always ashamed of it! Believe me, I tried not to do it. Sometimes I begged myself to stop, but I couldn't help myself. Name any bad feeling – shame, guilt, ugliness, failure – they hit me whenever I picked and I deserved every one of them!"

He closed his eyes again, pursing his lips as if in pain. "But goddamn it, those days are over! I've stopped kidding myself! This… " – he touched his nose again – "it aint just a habit. It's your… bottom line! Your character! It shows you what you're made of! Are you strong or weak, brave or cowardly, a God-fearing Christian or a hypocrite, a grown man or a spoiled brat? Where's your dignity, your self-respect, your discipline? One little thing in your nose, got to get rid of it right away? Scratch every itch, solve every problem, fix everything that bothers you? Why? Because you're spoiled, that's why! Because all your life you've been protected. Because you're a rich kid who never grew up. Because your mommy and daddy saw to it that anything wrong got fixed right away! Slightest discomfort in your nose – go after it! It aint supposed to be there! Momma's little prince aint supposed to be uncomfortable! Boogers are insults, blows to his pride!

"Well, sooner or later a man's got to face himself, and that's what I'm doing now. I'm done with being weak. From this moment on, my nose don't boss me around no more. Life aint comfortable, that's a fact. A man's alive, he's uncomfortable, is how I see it. Why should I be different? When things get tough, the tough get going, right? If you can't get tough with boogers, how you gonna handle Dick Cheney or Osama Bin Laden?

"Come right down to it, nose-picking aint nothing but addiction. Take it from an old drunk like me. Picking or drinking, no difference between them. Alcoholic, pickaholic – you running from your problems. Thirty seconds by yourself, bam, your finger's in your nose! Maybe nothing up there but you're looking for it anyway! Why? Because you're a goddamn drunk! You grab for your boogers like you grab for a drink! It's all the same! And who don't know that it aint just your nose that bosses you around? Every kind of bother, nuisance, irritation, every annoyance, aggravation, frustration, anything the least bit unpleasant – they're all boogers to you! The whole world, life itself – nothing but boogers! Ordinary guy, president of the

United States, draft-dodger, governor of Texas, don't matter who you are, you picking all the time!

"But if you're president, you aint so ordinary, are you? You got more boogers than anyone else and aint none of them easy to pick. Sometimes, face it, they can't be picked at all! Terrorism, budget crisis, hurricane, Global Warming… Saddam Hussein, Al Qaeda, Iran, Katrina – how you gonna pick 'em? If you can hang in with them instead of going after them right away, you're a statesman! If not, you got no business being president. Listen to me, America! I'm talkin' from my heart! All my fuck-ups in the White House weren't nothing but the work of a dumb-ass pickaholic! You think I invade Iraq if I'm no pickaholic? What was Saddam but another booger for me?"

For the most part, the controversy that followed this tirade was sadly superficial. Most opinion divided according to bias about the practice. AntiNasalists celebrated his "honesty" and "recovery" while those we've come to call "traditional practitioners" saw his "retreat" as a repetition of what one rhinologist called "the shallowness and puritanism that made him such a disaster as a president."[257] All this, as I say, was the easy response of those who were either new to the Path or fixed in superficial views of it. For deeper understanding, you had to search out the PostNasal blogs which, as I mention – and quote – in *The Complete Book of Nasalism*, were just at that time beginning to appear on the web. At Andreaj.com, for example, Andrea Jackson, a longtime student of Ettingoff, who'd been part of the first Klondyke experiments, wrote:

> "Like anyone else I'm disappointed with his condemnation of the practice, but if you read between the lines of his statement, you see he's not moving back but forward. He's not talking taste or etiquette, no fear of taboo or social ostracism. He's talking tolerance and discipline. Like a true

257 Hitchman, Dawkins. Letter to editor. *Extract* May 2011 "Why should we trust him now when he's never been trustworthy in his life?"

PostNasalist, he understands that crusts can tyrannize as well as motivate."[258]

And two days later, Robert Fawck agreed with her:

> "It's true that Bush didn't mention "patience" or "curiosity," but he is clearly embracing both. Let the reactionaries call him a puritan. Myself, I celebrate his breakthrough. George W. Bush is not rejecting Nasalism! He's consummating it!"[259]

But George wasn't finished. He lifted his hand from his chest and curled it into a fist. "Okay, America, there's my apology. What about yours? Look at yourself! Look at the man on your screen! Ask yourself how come you elected him. Re-elected him! How is it possible that at a time when you needed, more than ever, a president with maturity and wisdom, you chose a man with no experience, no qualifications, a dry-drunk pickaholic who showed you time and again that he wasn't up to the job! Terrorism! Global Warming! Economic crisis! Danger on all sides! Why is it that more than 50 million of you voted to put your destiny in my hands? I'll tell you why! You've got so much information coming at you that your head is spinning out of control! TV, movies, Internet, newspapers, magazines. You're under attack! Words and pictures all the time, opinions crashing against each other. Yes, no, good, bad. So much stuff in your head that you don't know up from down anymore. Can't think, can't remember! How you gonna know who's the right man for the job? No way! You go for the soundbyte. Listen to Karl Rove. Cut to the commercial. Because in the end you're pickaholics. Drunks or dry-drunks, just like me. Soundbytes are boogers! Commercials are boogers! TV is boogers! Aint it natural that when Election Day comes 'round, you chose a soundbyte? You know that's all I was. And it's all you wanted me to be. Face

---

258   Linchak, *The Complete Book of Nasalism*, op. cit., 1267.

259   Ibid.,1267

it, America. Everything is boogers for you! That's why I got elected! You went for the guy who thinks like you do, picks like you do, makes you feel the way you feel when your finger's in your nose!"

SIXTEEN

Throughout that day and the next, I emailed and left phone messages for him, but I got no answer. Stunned as I was by the vlog, I found myself unable to work and, like so many, watched it again and again on his website or its endless replays on TV or other websites, like YouTube and Nytimes.com, and, by means of Google and LexisNexis, followed the discussion and polling results it generated on the web and in the media.[260] My own blog, of course, joined the chorus and, since my friendship with him was widely mentioned, evoked its own response in the form of direct email replies,[261] quotes in the media, and, as he documented on his own blog, another flood of interview requests to my agent.[262]

Fortunately, I had an escape hatch. Weeks before, I had scheduled a trip to Cambridge to visit with Klondyke and Fawck at MIT. Three days after the vlog appeared, I took the early-morning shuttle. Settling into a bulkhead seat, I felt as if I'd found a paradise of quiet. I fastened my seat belt, set my laptop on the tray table, and, while I waited for boot-up, connected the video-headset which Sara had given me for my

260   Ibid., 1267–1269.

261   Ibid., 1268.

262   Conrad, Peter. Peterconrad.com, May 11, 2011.

last birthday. Earlier versions had been marketed but this was a state-of-the-art update which Microsoft had developed in collaboration with Murgate's Sony division. It had a 100MG hard drive and a folding external keyboard, so it could be used as a stand-alone computer, but I preferred to bypass its operating system, plug it into my laptop, and use its eyeglass screen as monitors. With LCD screens in each eyepiece and the most effective noise-canceling headphones on the market, it had finally made it possible for me to do serious work on a plane.

I had a backlog of research to deal with, but my first priority was a massive file on Fawck which Carlotta had forwarded just the day before. Given Fawck's eminence and the complexity and ambition of his work, I had to study it carefully in order to prepare for my meeting with him in Cambridge. Not that it lacked competition. Nothing ever does when you're doing research on the Internet. Sara had sent me new work on crust-adhesion from Tokyo University, and Carlotta had turned up two multi-tasking studies – from Leningrad's Rhinology Institute and a private neuroscience facility financed by Singapore industrialist, Ha Jhin Pho, which explored the effect of nose-picking on information-processing capacity and arrived at completely opposite results.[263] There were also, thanks to a forward by Ann Curtis just the day before, several articles (two by theologians, two by rhinologists, half a dozen by political journalists, and one which interviewed former cabinet members and other influential Republicans) on George's vlog. Sara's staff had forwarded polling results (Neilsen, Gallup, Roper, the Pew Charitable Trust, and Greenberg-Quinlan-Rosner) showing close to 100% negative or "outrage." Indeed, according to *USA Today* – in an article forwarded by Carlotta – George had produced "the first unanimous vote in polling history."[264]

---

263   The Russian work showed an increase of 15%, the work in Singapore, a loss of almost ten.

264   *USA Today*, June 15, 2011.

As the other passengers filed in, I clicked onto my email program and, as was my habit, sent a good morning IM to Sara.

"Where you?" she replied.

"Plane."

"Love me?"

"Of course."

"Me too."

"Fireworks in limo?"

"No. Sob. Never when I want it."

I lifted my eyeglasses. The aisle was full of passengers rolling bags behind them or wearing them on their backs. Of ten that passed me while I watched, six were on their cell phones and three wore headphones. Some had wires drooping across their chests, and some were wireless, only buds in their ears or hook-shaped devices that hung from their earlobes. When I looked again, she'd sent another IM.

"But many ways to come. Mega-twinge a while ago."

"Tell me."

"Tiny crust, mostly liquid, uncanny, tenacious. Like rooted in my head! Hard work to get it but release my God electric."

"Adhesion. Who understands it?"

"Did you read the Tokyo research I sent you?"

"Not yet. Why?"

"That's just what they're investigating."

Opening my email, I found forty-five messages. Thirty were spam and five had manuscripts attached – three from former students and two from well-known writers, both friends, who wanted blurbs. There was also, at last, an answer from George.

He asked my forgiveness – with a sad caveat. "It's true I'm off picking, but if it weren't for you, I'd still be in the clinic. You know I'm grateful."

Searching for more, I dashed off an IM – "Are you online? Where are you? And how?" – but got no reply. After waiting a moment, I turned at last to my file on Fawck. It loaded quickly from Carlotta's attachment but its first line directed me to his website. I went online through the wireless connection on the plane, then clicked on the link in Carlotta's message. While waiting for it to load, another IM from Sara appeared on-screen. "Do you know Hawkinson?"

"No. Who is he?"

"Just found him, sent you his page. J.T. Hawkinson. Texas A&M. Adhesion again. Google him. Better than the Tokyo stuff, I think."

I raised my glasses. The doors of the plane had just been closed and the stewardesses were checking seat backs and seat belts. The news was on the television overhead. A blond weatherwoman with ghoulish makeup and bags under her eyes, recited with a hysterical smile while pointing to a radar map. News items, stock quotes, and a closed-caption version of her recitation ran along the bottom of the screen.

A stocky, round-faced African American woman had taken the seat beside me. She looked to be in her early thirties. She had huge eyes, luminous black skin, hair pulled tight in a bun the size of a cantaloupe, and a yin-yang tattoo on her left forearm. She gasped when she saw me. "Oh my God, it's you! Forgive me. I'm an admirer. Especially *9/11*."

I thanked her, lowered my glasses, opened Sara's email, and followed the link she'd sent – Hawkinson.org. The first link on the home page was to data produced by the work in Tokyo. The home page was all numbers and equations. A quick scan was all I managed before I sent it on to Carlotta.

As the plane backed out of the gate, I finally turned to Fawck. He'd published nine books, two on philosophy, two on neuroscience, and the other five on their integration, the specialty in which he'd achieved his eminence, neurophilosophy. Carlotta had sent brief synopses of each. His articles – many of them summarized by her as well – had appeared in either philosophical, neuroscience, or neurophilosophical journals as well as popular media such as *Scientific American*, *New England Journal of Medicine*, and *Nature*. A profile of him, which she'd attached in full, had appeared in *The New York Times Magazine* in April 2002. In recent years, as he'd become more interested in rhinology, he'd become something of an authority on brain-imaging. His blog, which he'd published steadily since 2001, covered all these subjects as well as, of course, nose-picking. Carlotta had also sent short biographies from the *Encyclopedia Britannica* and finally, this one, from Wikipedia.

> "Studied the neurosciences while pursuing his doctorate in philosophy. As comfortable in the lab as in the classroom, a rarity among neurophilosophers in being equally respected by both sides of the specialty. Said to be as good as any neuroradiologist at administering and reading brain-scans.[265]

Complete though it was, the Wiki had omitted important details which Carlotta noted in separate attachments, this one from *Rhinotillexis*,

> "Most of his colleagues believe that his ideas evolved out of his amazing mix of knowledge and experience, but his blog has more than once attributed them to nose-picking."[266]

And this one, from the most recent issue of *The Annals of Rhinology*,

> "Early studies with Klondyke, using brain-scans, have shown deactivations in the frontal lobe when extraction is in progress, proving, he says, that 'nose-picking neutralizes desire by focusing it on objects devoid of meaning.' Often criticized for such hypotheses but doesn't back down. As he writes in April 14, 2004 blog, "Every time I put my finger in my nose, I experience freedom from desire."[267]

---

265 "Robert Fawck," Wikipedia.com.

266 Klondyke, *Rhinotillexis*, op. cit., 112.

267 Norris, Peter. "Fawck moves on," *The Annals of Rhinology* Vol. 384 (May 2011) 23–45.

As meteorologist Melvin Lazarov demonstrates in his humidity research,[268] airplane cabins – dry as they are, hyper-oxygenated, and full of people with what Mickey, in one of his virulent anti-nasal blogs, once called "the principal motivation for nose-picking," idle hands[269] – are comparable to Rhinobate in the aggression and size of the crusts they engender. At that time, of course, I'd not seen the Lazarov data (Ann Curtis would forward it to me a few days later), but having noted the phenomenon myself, I wasn't surprised by a sudden appearance, in my left nostril, of the sensation – a perfectly balanced mix of excitement and discomfort – that even PostNasalists find exciting. Like most airplane crusts, it was clearly encapsulated ("autonomous," in the Klondyke vernacular[270]) from the beginning. It ought to have been a simple no-problem extraction but instead of inserting, I found what Fawck has called "the patience gap"[271] awaiting me once again. If I hadn't yet closed the Third Gate, I'd not backed off from it either. I did not want to pick and did not mind that I did not and, with regard to my state of mind, felt neither apprehensive nor self-critical.

---

268 Lazarov, Melvin. *Humidity and the Brain* (New York: Basic Books, 2004). It should be noted that Lazarov's view is controversial. Psychologist Nathan Frederick (in a passionate response to Lazarov's blog on February 16, 2006) laid airplane crusts entirely to claustrophobia, while immunologist Dorothy Wathover (Wathover892.com), answering both Lazarov and Frederick on Lazarov's blog two days after Frederick weighed in, agreed with Mickey but took his view to a further depth by arguing that "idle hands" cause "an immune response which in itself generates nasal secretion." Needless to say, any view of this controversy must include Prezl and his elegant adhesion equations which relate both fingertip-adhesion and membrane-adhesion to humidity, not to mention Crimmins' view that "the ideal crust will perfectly balance the Prezl equation, with equal attachment to the fingertip and the membrane, thus producing maximum suspense before extraction and ultimate twinge at release." (See Crimmins, David."Ideal Crusts," *Extract* March 2013: 19–34. Bayer scientists have credited both Prezl and Crimmins for assisting in the development of their Tillexinhaler which was recently rated, by *Consumer Reports* (October 2013), first among crust-producers.

269 Linchak, Mickey. Micklinchak.com, March 11, 2012.

270 Klondyke, Marcus. *Rhinotillexis Third Edition* (New York: Murgate, 2013) 1245.

271 Fawck, *PostNasal and Beyond*, op. cit., 21–24.

It's no surprise I thought of George at that moment. All his life, he'd confessed to me once, he'd suffered from impatience, but clearly, in his tolerance for crusts, he'd arrived at the sort of equanimity I felt just now. How else explain the wisdom and courage – the amazing honesty – he'd shown on the vlog? How could I doubt that such maturity, affecting me as it had affected him, would make me a better writer? Of course I knew nothing at that time about the research connecting language and crusts,[272] hypographia and idio-picking,[273] but even if I had, the memory of George's vlog would have saved me from pessimism.

I lifted my glasses. We were waiting in line for takeoff. I'm sure the captain had offered an explanation for the delay but my headphones so muffled external noise that I'd not heard his announcement. News continued on the TV overhead, a male anchorman now, and type continuing its incessant parade across the bottom of the screen. Since the New York stock market had not yet opened, Tokyo prices were offered. It was cold and raining – 38 degrees – in Boston, snowing and 27 in Chicago, sunny and 76 in LA. The major news was a murder in Connecticut, a mudslide in Guatemala, and, as had been a constant since the vlog, the fact that George had disappeared. "Family and friends report no sign of ex-President" marched below images of the mudslide. Abruptly, the news was replaced by flight information. Flying time to Boston, weather in Boston, flying altitude, etc. Choices available for breakfast and snacks. Then: "US Air is proud to announce its new entertainment system: twelve music channels, four comedy channels, and one hundred forty-five video channels." In addition to re-runs of network and cable programs, one could choose among seventy-five movies, eighteen videogames, and, of course, by means of the wireless connection I'd just utilized, avail oneself of the entire range of Internet surfing options.

---

272 Linchak, *The Complete Book of Nasalism*, op. cit., 674.

273 Ibid., 857.

Though more and more irritating, the crust remained entirely a matter of curiosity which itself, to an extent that seemed almost miraculous, diminished my discomfort. Nevertheless, giving into what Janice Wier, in a wonderful PhD thesis – "Ritualized Nasalism" – she did for Klondyke in 2009, calls "Pavlovian Picking,"[274] I wiped my finger on the underside of the armrest, realizing an instant later that there was nothing to wipe off. As Weir explains, "For longtime practitioners, whose practice is highly ritualized, the phantom crust is no less vivid than the real."[275]

The young woman in the adjacent seat was watching me intently. Her eyes were bright and earnest. She had a habit of dropping her eyebrows and closing her left eye that made her look like she was trolling for information. Between her feet was an open leather briefcase containing two books and a thickness of magazines. The books were a recently issued new translation of *Anna Karenina* and a paperback by Ray Kurzwell, *The Age of the Spiritual Machine*. On her lap was an open copy of *The New Yorker* and, folded beneath it, *The Nation*, *Harper's*, and *The New York Times*. While she read, she held a miniature scanner in her right hand, tracing lines she wanted to retain. I owned the same model myself. It stored four gigabytes and downloaded through a USB cable which also recharged its battery. After a moment, she reached into her briefcase, removed a cell phone, brought it close to her mouth, and spoke into it softly. I owned one of these as well. It was state-of-the-art technology, a recently marketed combination of a cell phone, a BlackBerry, and an all-purpose Digital Assistant which was about the size of a package of cigarettes. It was currently residing, fully-charged and activated, in the inside pocket of my jacket. I kept it switched on, for the most part, because in addition to being a phone, a camera, a

---

274   Weir, Janice. "Ritualized Picking" (PhD thesis, Oral Roberts University, 2014). Published first on Rhinotillexis.com and then by Little, Brown, 2015.

275   Ibid., 134.

video player, and, of course, a wireless Internet utility, it was an audio recorder. What was really great about it was that it could be programmed to log on at regular intervals and automatically email its audio file. I'd been using it since *9/11* to forward my interviews, notes, and recorded audio files to Carlotta, myself, and Sara. Since it kept its charge for twelve hours or more and could store up to nine hours of audio, I had a habit of keeping it activated on work-related trips, using it, for all intents and purposes, as a two-way radio. Just now it was set to log on and email its files every fifteen minutes. Thus, by the time my plane landed in Boston, most of what I'd said or heard or noted on the plane would be on Sara's and Carlotta's computers. Furthermore, since both had voice-recognition software which converted to print with high accuracy, the whole of the email would be translated to text on their word processors.

The pilot announced that we were cleared for takeoff and directed the flight crew to take their seats. After a quick scan of Carlotta's notes and those of my own which I'd appended to them, I closed the Fawck file. I clicked on *The New York Times* to see if there was any news on George and, finding nothing but the same headline I'd seen on TV a few minutes before, I went to his website to watch the vlog again. He was just into his first confession – "I'm here to tell you that this was untrue" – when I smelled coffee. The breakfast cart was moving through the aisle. I removed my glasses, took my laptop off the tray-table, and accepted the tray the stewardess offered. Banana, bagel, orange juice, coffee. Accepting her own tray, the woman in the adjacent seat turned to me. "Forgive me for intruding. I have to tell you I'm a writer myself."

I was not uninterested in her or, for that matter, my breakfast, but I was facing now another result of the PostNasal Gap. Nourished by the atmosphere in the cabin, the crust had grown so large that it had almost completely blocked my nostril. As anyone knows, obstructed breath completely dwarfs focal irritation when it comes to levels of discomfort. In fact, my breath by now was totally asymmetrical. The solution, of course, was to blow my nose, but like so many practitioners, Nasal as well as PostNasal, I had great resistance to doing so.[276] Many bemoan[277] and some pathologize[278] this constraint. Like so much else about this practice, it is at once avoided and unavoidable. Surely, we ought by now to treat it with compassion. For Nasalists, blowing wastes extractions and eliminates the twinge. For PostNasalists, it interrupts patience and distracts curiosity. How can we be surprised that Oprah Winfrey, on the show that featured the acrimonious debate between Klondyke and Fawck, was so moved by their agreement on this matter that she referred to blowing as "heretical?"[279] Please don't think that, when I speak of compassion, I'm being lyrical or romantic. I'm only acknowledging impossible contradiction, a case in which temptation and anathema are equally intense. Just now, for example, my nostril so blocked that it was beginning to whistle on the inhale, a paper napkin had come with my breakfast tray. With a sense almost of recklessness, I raised the napkin to my nose and gave myself over to wholehearted discharge. As often with dense, encapsulated crusts, relief was so quick and unqualified that it produced feelings close to extraction itself.

276　Two recent surveys have explored this unsurprising phenomenon with remarkably similar results. In a questionaire distributed to students at four Ivy League colleges, Yale rhinologist, Reginald Surrey, found that, of 2,547 who answered "yes" to the question, "Do you consider yourself a Nasalist?" 1,675 considered "avoidance of blowing" to be "preferable," and 1,245 called it "a necessity." (Surrey, Reginald. *Yale Medical Journal* Vol. 2356 (April 2013) 25–34. Asking the same questions in a nationwide survey, Harriet Leach, medical director of the Gay and Lesbian Health Initiative found that 12,546 or 37% of those calling themselves "persistent pickers" avoided blowing "whenever possible." (Leach, Harriet. *Gay And Lesbian Newsletter* April 19, 2012).

277　Chalmers, R.K. "Resistance to Blowing: Discipline or Phobia?" *Extract* June 3, 2013: 321–346.

278　Anyan, Ravi. "Inhibitions and Prohibitions," *International Journal of Fear* May 1, 2010: 23–98.

279　"Oprah," August 15, 2013.

With no little amazement, I noticed that I was without regret for my behavior. For an instant, in fact, I knew the "pure mix of contentment and exhilaration" which, as Mickey once said on his television show, "awaits anyone who can 'blow off' the endless confusion that Nasalism generates."[280]

Despite the fact that I'd not sneezed, the woman said, "Bless you!" and I said, "Thanks." Amazing, isn't it, how often behavior which originates in the nose will tap the habits and rituals of etiquette and socialization. What is better than exchanges of this sort for opening doors to conversation? I offered her my hand, and asked her name. Louise LeFlore, it was. She lived on Cape Cod, wrote fiction and non-fiction and features for local newspapers. She said she'd read everything I'd written. Still, she repeated, *9/11* was her favorite. "Would it be possible to send you a copy for an autograph?"

It's no surprise that I felt as if I knew her. I'd just had, in the seat next to her, an exhilarating experience. I speak not only of blowing, of course. For the first time in my life, I had experienced unambivalent patience. "Don't be silly. Give me your address and I'll sign a copy and send it to you."

"Oh my God!" she cried. "How sweet!"

Evacuation incomplete, "Excuse me," I said, and blew again.

"Bless you," she said again, and I again, "Thanks."

"Are you okay?" she said.

"Fine, thanks."

"I've been reading your nose-picking blogs."

I wadded the napkin and, coffee finished, stuffed it into my empty cup.

"Nothing scares you, does it? How many writers on your level are willing to take such risks? I told my editor about you. He asked me to do a piece on the blogs."

She explained that she was a college administrator by

---

280   "Dr. Mickey," Lifetime Network, January 19, 2012.

profession, assistant dean at a non-resident institution called Cape Cod University, in Truro, Massachusetts. She wrote fiction and poetry and, for spare change, criticism and features for *The Cape Cod Times* and *The Provincetown Banner.* "Movies, TV, art, or, like the piece I'm doing on your blogs, stuff I pick up on the web." She dug a wallet out of her briefcase and offered me her card.

"Cape Cod U," I said. "They write every year to offer me a job."

"It was probably me who wrote. We're always looking for prestige. Young as we are, we need all the help we can get. A writer like you is worth a fortune to us. If you read one or two manuscripts, we can feature you in our ads. No telling how much they'd pay you for that."

"They?"

"Time, Inc. They bought us last year. Needless to say, it changed our situation. They've raised our salary scale and upgraded our computers. Why should they not? We're a cash cow for them. Minimal investment, 30% profit margin, great PR."

I'd read articles about Cape Cod U and other non-resident colleges. *The Times*, *The Atlantic*, and *The New Yorker* had all done features on them recently, and *The New York Times Book Review* had recently reviewed several books about them. They were correspondence schools of a sort which had become more and more common of late. Communicating by fax, email, or videophone, students and teachers rarely met face-to-face. Of course, the great advantage of an institution like this was that it required almost no real estate. Although Cape Cod U, for example, operated out of a two-story house on a dirt road in a town which had no supermarket, restaurant, or pharmacy, its computers and satellite connections allowed it to serve students all over the world.

"How many students do you have?"

"A little under 30,000. Faculty close to 4,000. In other words, seven students for every teacher."

"What's the curriculum?"

"Writing and painting, for the most part. Sculpture too, of course. Filmmaking, a lot of video. We're mainly about writers though. At last count, 64% of our students were writers. Manuscripts are emailed, and teachers are obligated, by contract, to respond within two weeks. On average, a teacher deals with two manuscripts per student per semester. In the seven years we've been in business, we've produced more than 8,000 novels. 193 published! We average like 200 filmscripts a year. Short stories, poetry, non-fiction books. I can't recall the numbers. One of our screenwriters won Sundance last year!"

On the PA system, the pilot announced that we'd reached our cruising altitude.

"You've got to excuse me," I said. "Work to do before we land."

I put on my glasses and went online again. I had thought to review the Fawck information but on impulse decided to watch the vlog again. On my way to it, however, a Google headline announced "BUSH ASSASSINATION RUMORS." I double-clicked on it and it took me to *The New York Times* website.

> "Rumors about the whereabouts of ex-President George W. Bush, who hasn't been seen or heard from for the last three days, are circulating on the Internet. According to the *Huffington Post*, he was seen yesterday in Amman, Jordan. Another witness, quoted in *The New York Post*, reports seeing him board a plane in Houston. Finally, a blogger has reported 'irrefutable evidence' that the FBI is investigating a right-wing plot against Mr. Bush – vengeance for what many have called his 'anti-American' remarks on his vlog."

An IM from Sara appeared, superimposed on the *Times'* website. "U hear rumor?"

"Just now," I wrote. "The *Times*."

"It's all over TV."

"True, U think?"

"Who knows? So much bullshit flying around. U trace blog?"

"Which?"

"One who says right-wing plot."

"Who he?"

"Wait, I'll get address."

A moment later, she sent it along, and I clicked on it. Though better written and more specific than the usual blogossip, it offered little more than the article which had brought me to it. Realizing I wanted the link – whether it was true or not – in my files, I opened my email program and sent both it and the *Times* article to Sara and myself. Then I went back to Google and entered "Bush assassination" in the search-box. I wasn't surprised to find the Times article listed first or, further down, the blog and the *Huffington Post* article. Even the 12,346 references listed in the Google tally below seemed more or less predictable.[281] What caught my eye was a link further down on the first page: DEATH ON LARRY KING. I clicked on it and found myself on YouTube. Here was the first of what would become a flood of videos depicting George's death. Facing Larry King again, asking again for a close-up so that he could be seen inserting, he looked into the camera and raised his finger to his nose. Before he could insert, however, a pistol entered from the left side of the screen and fired into his temple. Familiar though I was with the surreal inventions of digital editing and special-effect technology, I was horrified by the detail of the image. The sight of his head being torn asunder was so real that, especially in slow motion, it was almost impossible to doubt.

According to Technorati.com, this video had already – less than 48 hours after its posting – been viewed by more than

---

281   As Edward Hirshenson reports in *Bush Online* (New York: Harcourt, Brace, 2012), this number grew to more than 17 million within 48 hours.

17 million people. Within a week, its audience would exceed one hundred million, within six months, a billion. Even so, its popularity is nowhere near that of the doctored video in which Dick Cheney is shown holding the gun that kills Bush or any of the half-dozen videos in which he commits suicide.

The clock on my laptop showed 8:17. I watched the YouTube video twice and was about to watch it again when the stewardess tapped me on the shoulder. Just ten minutes late, the plane was descending, the lights of Boston spread out below. I sent the assassination video to Sara and Carlotta, then signed off the net, removed my glasses, closed my laptop, and slipped it into its case. Louise had closed *The New Yorker* and packed all her reading material into her briefcase. Across the aisle, a teenage girl was watching the assassination video on her iPhone. On the TV above me, the screen was split, a male anchorman on one side, a female on the other. A title at the bottom of the screen reported 234 deaths in the Guatemala mudslide. Finally, the bottom line showed the time and the temperature in Boston.

As the plane touched down, Louise said, "Can I ask a favor of you?"

"Sure."

"Can I take our picture?"

"Why not?"

She took out her cell phone, held it at arm's length above and between us, then snapped the picture.

"Will you send it to me?"

"Sure. Give me your address."

Tapping buttons, she entered my address, then tapped a few more to send the picture. Next time I checked my email, I found it waiting for me. Two weeks later, using the same email address, she sent me the article she'd written about my blogs. It featured the same photograph.

SEVENTEEN

MIT's Rhinology Department was located on the twelfth and thirteenth floors of a non-descript high-rise in a residential neighborhood about half a block from the main campus. I called from the lobby, and Klondyke met me at the elevator.

Though we'd met but once, just a few days before, he greeted me as if we were old friends. He took my arm and led me down the hall to his office. It was a chaos of paper, books, charts, and exotic instrumentation. His lab was next door to it, separated by a wall of bookshelves built around a large window which was actually, as I'd discover, a one-way mirror through which he viewed his subjects while he scanned them. Opposite the mirror was a huge wooden desk on which he'd cleared a path between his books and papers to lay out a generous breakfast spread for us. To the left of the desk, mounted on a rotating pedestal, was a cream-colored model of a human nose about four feet in height (**Appendix B**). Showing it off was his first order of business.

"Touch it," he said.

Its skin was elastic, a silicone rubber that looked and felt completely real, inside and out. Its nostrils were close to a foot apart, each about three inches in diameter. Several of its interior sections were exposed because its outside walls were hinged and motor driven, activated by a remote-control device which he proceeded now to demonstrate for me. Aiming it at the open nostril, he pressed a button which controlled a chain of white lights below the turbinate. Each button-press activated a different light but pressing it twice activated all of them. Complicated and beautiful, the internal nasal anatomy was now exposed. The sinus cavities were bright red, the so-called "turbinates" – where sinus fluid, he explained, enters from cavities in the brain – turquoise, the sinus canal black and twisted like a river on a map. Activating the chain of lights, he explained, "This is the movement of secretion, emerging here from the turbinate, and descending under the influence, among other things, of the cilia." Pressing another button, he turned off the white lights and turned on a red one, high on the septum. "And this is mucus coagulating, developing into a crust."

If you've read *The Complete Book of Nasalism*, you've seen the annotated picture of this model. It is illustration number 17, page 116. Directly or indirectly, it is mentioned with relevance in footnote numbers 256, 308, and 345. It was the product of collaboration between Klondyke and a Brazilian sculptor, Manuel Olivados,[282] who for the last two years had been a visiting professor in the art department. Harriet Van Pelt, an associate professor in MIT's Department of Computer Engineering, had developed its software. It was already in the pipeline for a US patent which, when granted two years later, would make it a cash cow for its inventors and, of course, MIT, which shared ownership of all patents developed by its faculty. These days, a version not so different from the one I saw in the office that day is used in rhinology and otolaryngology departments at universities and medical schools all over the world. A smaller model, with Microsoft Xbox software, is available for the home. Indeed, appealing as it does to teenagers as well as adults, it is said to be one of the more popular video games on the market now.

---

282 Olivados' recent show at Knoedler in New York features large bronze figures of noses viewed internally and externally.

On the wall behind his desk hung a print of an illustration – showing a diagram of nasal anatomy with a finger poised before the nose – which had appeared on the cover of *Rhinotillexis* (**Figure 14**) and, next to it, in a black metal frame, a four-foot-by-seven-foot print of the Bernstein photograph I'd seen before on the conference brochure. With no little pride, he explained that (as I knew already from the brochure) this was an 8 which he himself had extracted. She had taken the picture just four months earlier. Iconic and monumental, the crust was at least three feet in diameter. Influenced by the gigantic photographs of Gursky and Misrach, Bernstein had just begun to investigate enlargements of this size. She was already well known but, as *The New York Times* would write after her 2009 breakthrough show at New York's Pace/MacGill Gallery, "One cannot doubt that these prints will cement her reputation."[283]

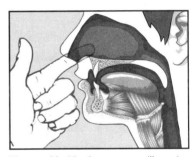

Figure 14 Nasal anatomy illustration which has appeared on the cover of the first and second editions of *Rhinotillexis* as well as the audiobook (New York: Sony Audio, 2012), the CD-ROM (New York: Murgate Entertainment, 2012), and the DVDs of both the Nasalism documentary and the American Masters program, "Marcus Klondyke," broadcast initially on PBS, September 2013. In a program financed by Rupert Murdoch, major shareholder of Murgate, T-shirts bearing this image are distributed on Christmas every year to American troops in Iraq.

He'd set out a bowl of fruit and lox and bagels and cream cheese for us.

As we sat down to eat, I asked if Fawck would be joining us. Since they worked together and all their papers were signed by both of them, I'd expected that he'd be part of this meeting.

Clearly uncomfortable, Klondyke shook his head. "I invited him, but he declined. He wants you to call him, come down to his office after you leave

---

283 *The New York Times*, May 19, 2009.

here." He opened a drawer in his desk and brought out a bag of coffee. "Decaf or regular?"

"Regular," I said.

With a bright red state-of-the-art machine on the table beneath the diagram, he made separate cups for us. "Professor Fawck is the reason I'm here, you know. He's the reigning superstar on the faculty. If you've read his blogs, you know that his passion for rhinotillexis is equal to mine. When he pushed for my appointment, he got their attention. We've been friends and colleagues since the day I arrived, but lately, our research priorities seem to be diverging."

"Can you say why?"

"I think you'd best ask him about that. All I can tell you is that most everyone around here finds him difficult these days. And he seems to feel the same way about us."

When we finished eating, he took me into the small room adjacent to his office which he viewed through the mirror-window opposite his desk. I saw now for the first time his brain imaging machine, the so-called Rhinomag (**Figure 15**). I'd seen photos of it and read about it, of course, on Rhinotillexis.com and in a recent article on the work which he and Fawck had completed together in *Scientific American*, but seeing it for real evoked feelings near to awe in me. It was a mobile, compact version of a state-of-the-art functional magnetic resonance imaging device. Once a technology which required that patients be wired to an array of EEG cables (**Figure 16**), it was now, thanks to the recent dramatic miniaturization of most of its components, simplified and reconfigured so that all its imaging technology was contained in a steel cone which encircled and gripped a patient's head. Beneath the cone was an orange recliner with three gleaming stainless steel trays attached on movable armatures. Cables emerged from the arms of the chair as well as its pedestal. Attached by an armature to the wall, the cone exuded its own miasma of cables. On a desk to the left of the chair was

Figure 15 *Rhinomag.*

Compact nasal scanner invented by Klondyke and Harris Meacham, professor of medical engineering at MIT, in collaboration with Dorothy Daniels of MicroSoft and Andra Samelson, director of photovoltaic research at General Electric. Like all functional magnetic resonance imaging devices, it uses a powerful magnetic field, radio waves, and a computer to measure metabolic changes that take place in the nose, the hand, fingers, and, of course, active parts of the brain. It then produces detailed pictures which are examined on a computer monitor, printed, or, of course, electronically mailed.

a keyboard, a large flat-screen monitor, and a laser printer, all of which of course were linked to the MIT server which was located in a secure, protected facility half a mile away.

While he busied himself at the keyboard, Klondyke directed me to sit in the recliner. Pressing keys, he tilted it and extended its footrest so as to raise my feet and lean it toward the rear. He pulled on a pair of plastic gloves and, explaining each as he connected them, wired up the diagnostic leads the Rhinomag contained. "In addition to imaging brain actitity, it tracks your EEG and your eye movements, fixation, and pupil diameter as well as, of course, trigeminal excitation."

All such information, he explained, was transmitted wirelessly to the MIT mainframe which, in turn, processed, stored, and backed up data in triplicate,

Figure 16   *EEG.*
    Peter Felsenheis, Klondyke's first subject, participating in initial rhinotillexis research at John Hopkins. Before his lab had access to brain scan technology, lacking the means by which to measure trigeminal activation or neurological activity, Klondyke asked subjects to record subjective crust experience by means of computer. Though dwarfed by information gained through the Rhinomag, this early data is frequently referenced by contemporary rhinologists. Indeed, Klondyke himself has often called Felsenheis "the first Nasalist."

then uploaded it to the department's website and emailed it to those on their mailing list – faculty and researchers at MIT and other universities, as well as those who'd connected to them by way of the Internet.

When at last I was fully connected, he gave me a cotton swab and a small glass container with a plastic top and a label on which was printed my name, the date, the time, and a bar code which, of course, was already, with my name and birth date, recorded on the mainframe. A separate label on the container read: MIT RHINOLOGY. The container was for storage of what he called "extract." Explaining that "crust data" – glutination, weight, volume, viscosity, etc. – was essential to the study ("We've seen extremely interesting correlation, for example, between the molecular composition of a crust and firing in both the caudate and the nucleus accumbens."), he asked me to scrape my extraction into the container which, he explained, would be transferred as soon as possible to a small refrigerator[284] before it was taken to the lab for weighing, photographing, and, of course, chemical and molecular analysis.

"Which finger," he asked, "do you generally use?"

I raised both forefingers.

"Right or left?"

"Depends on the nostril, doesn't it?"

"You'd be surprised how many use the same hand no matter which nostril they pick. Anyway, intravenous Rhinobate is usually symmetrical. Right or left – it's up to you."

"Let's go with the right."

"So the left is our control."

He slipped a thick black leather glove on my left hand. "Electrodermal activity is collected by the processor in this glove. It has electrodes on the tips of the index and third finger and, like all our peripherals, transmits its data to the mainframe."

Removing a moistened tissue from a small plastic packet, he wiped my right forefinger. His hands were gentle, almost tender. "Comfortable?" he said.

"Very."

"Thirsty? Water?"

"No thanks."

"Orange juice?"

---

284 Needless to say, refrigerated crusts must be microwaved in order to be completely reconstituted.

"No."

"Tissue? Blow?"

"No, thanks. I'm fine."

Dipping another swab into another solution – mentholated, in this case – he cleaned my nostrils. Finally, from a drawer in the cabinet behind him, he removed the nose cup, which was, of course, the central weapon in his wireless arsenal. He attached it carefully so that it straddled my nostrils, tightened it with a small clamp on its exterior, then tapped it on the left and right. "There are 1,487 sensors in this cup. They give us an accurate read-out of all intranasal activity – chemical and electrical, epidermal, vascular, speed and volume of secretion, etcetera, etcetera."

As you may know from the rush of advertising which accompanied its release last year, the nose cup has been combined with the glove he'd placed on my left hand to form the "haptic interface" on which the video game called *Virtual Picking*[285] is based. I did not know it then, of course, but the interface was already in development by the haptic division in MIT's Computer Science Department. Combining cursor movement with intra-nasal sensation by means of communication between the glove, the cup, and a nostril imaged internally on-screen, *Virtual Picking* makes it possible to generate secretion, produce a crust, attach it to the membrane, and finally, extracting it without touching one's nose, experience what Microsoft calls "all the pleasure of full-blown rhinotillexis."

I told Klondyke that I wanted more information on the cup.

"Sure. I'll email its specs to you later. Is it too tight?"

"No."

"Too loose?"

"No, it seems okay."

---

285 *Virtual Picking*. Microsoft Xbox, 2010. First marketed in 2009. Updated in 2014 and again last year.

He sat at the desk and worked at his keyboard again. "Our software," he explained, "sets up your file with a photograph and all relevant biographical and rhinological information. All your data will be downloaded and processed."

He filled a syringe with Rhinobate, tied a rubber tourniquet around my arm, tapped for a vein, and inserted the needle when he found it. "Rhinobate is faster and more effective intravenously. Secretion in ninety seconds, max. Mature crust, ten to twelve minutes, sometimes nine or even eight. Initial sensation, four or five. You can talk to me if you like. There's an open mike to a speaker in my office. I'll be watching through the window of course. I can talk to you too. Any questions?"

"Breathe through my mouth?"

"No need for that. There's an oxygen line to the cup."

He sat at the keyboard again. I heard a series of keystrokes, three chimes, and a single musical chord. The cone descended slowly until it sat loosely on my head. I heard more keystrokes, more chimes. Then I felt the rubber collar within the cone tighten around my head.

"Okay?" he said.

"Okay," I said.

"See you later," he said.

He left the room and closed the door behind him. As he'd predicted, I felt symmetrical pressure in less than four minutes.[286] The crusts expanded in parallel, as if connected with each other. I'd done my share of oral Rhinobate but as he'd said, it was a different drug injected. Administered in this fashion, it so intensifies sensation that, as Jason Collins writes in his recent *Rhinobate Diaries*, it produces "a sort of hysteria in

---

[286] Collins, Jason. *Rhinobate Diaries* (New York: Murgate, 2011). As Collins notes, this early version of Rhinobate, producing crusts of unpredictable adhesion, was somewhat crude. Newer versions and, even more, Merck's synthetic Rhinobate, control this variable.

the nostril."[287] What followed for me was a combination of disorientation and trauma. With ordinary crusts, emergence was gradual and subtle, but these were aggressive, almost intimidating, "not a little," writes Collins, "like insects invading one's nostrils."[288]

Despite my recent experience with PostNasal patience, my response to these sensations was impatient or, as some might say, classical Nasalism.[289] In fact, my need to extract was, if anything, more fierce than any I'd known in the past.

But still, I did not surrender to it. My hand did not move. The PostNasal leap had happened and I was no longer equivocal about it. In other words, the Third Gate had closed behind me and, for reasons that Fawck explains better than anyone else,[290] its effect on my brain was irreversible. Tempted though I was by visions of relief, my curiosity about discomfort was so much more powerful than discomfort itself that I was steadfast, waiting out irritation with the sort of patience which only those feel whose brains are stripped of its opposite. Even more extraordinary, I knew for the first time what may be the greatest of all the gifts of PostNasalism: *the waiting that has no goal.*[291] I wasn't waiting for anything. I was *just waiting.*[292] And as so many have pointed out, this opened the door to a succession of revelations that dwarfed any I'd known before. Anyone who doubts that such a flood of insight could come from this experience need only check out recent brain imaging

---

287   Ibid., 234–256. "Anyone who's used this miraculous drug cannot be surprised that it was banned by the DEA though the FDA, true to form, has recently approved Nasalex, the Merck drug which is its exact synthetic replica. Nor can one be surprised that in the wake of its prohibition, an extensive black market has developed."

288   Ibid., 23.

289   Klondyke, *Rhinotillexsis Updated*, op. cit., 236.

290   Fawck, *PostNasal and Beyond*, op. cit., 13.

291   Ibid.

292   Ibid.

research – in Belfast,[293] Mexico City,[294] or here, in this very lab at MIT[295] – which demonstrates, again and again, the effects of patience on the cortical brain. Among other things, I understood that the peace I knew at this moment was what I'd been seeking since the first of my breakthrough crusts. Wasn't "concentration," after all, a kind of patience? And wasn't patience the ultimate freedom from discomfort? How could I be surprised that I wasn't picking or that, for the first time in months, I heard the Founder speaking to me again?

Talking from the office, where he'd been watching through the mirror, Klondyke's voice came from the speaker overhead.

"Finished?"

"I think so."

Returning a moment later, he sat at the keyboard and entered commands which caused the collar to loosen and the cone to rise. Then he busied himself disconnecting the diagnostic leads. Finally, he removed the nose cup, offered me a glass of water, and handed me a plastic bag which, like the container he'd given me before, was labeled with my name, the bar code, and the official insignia: "MIT RHINOLOGY."

"Blow into this, please."

With relief which surpassed even that which I'd felt on the plane, I squeezed the plastic against my nostrils and did as he'd asked.

He closed the bag, sealed it with a yellow tie, and stowed it in the refrigerator. "We call this 'secondary product.' There's a group in Prague who study it exclusively. The way they see it, blowing is mucus-driven, period. In other words, it was only the nature of your crusts that stopped you from extracting just now. Certain crusts, according to them, won't be extracted no

293   Linchak, *The Complete Book of Nasalism*, op. cit., 1254.

294   Ibid.

295   Ibid.

matter how irritating they are. They haven't published yet, but their work is on the web. I'll forward it to you if you like. We think they're crazy, but they're not lightweights."

He sat down at the keyboard again. A moment later, I heard the beeps and chimes, and then, for the first time, the printer. He studied the pages it produced, then rose from his chair. "As far as I can see, your crusts were unremarkable. Typical rhinobatoids. On the right .065, on the left .06 or .59. Trigeminal activation 6.67. Significant irritation, needless to say. Volume obstructive, pressure aggressive, but not a hint of activation in the motor centers of your brain or, from what I saw on your scan, the ventral striatum, which as you know, I'm sure, is the area associated with reward. In my view, you've got psychological issues with nose-picking. We call it tillexophobia. We're seeing it more and more often with advanced practitioners. It's not surprising. As you yourself have noted in your blogs, embracing the habit creates self-consciousness which is not only inhibiting but antithetical to the original impulse. After all, it's the freedom from self-consciousness that makes the habit so comforting in its early stages. There's an interesting article by your brother, Mickey, in the new issue of the *Lacan Journal*, where he says that rhinotillexis is primarily an act of dissociation.[296] You might remember that I suggested much the same in my book. There's no question that the awareness we develop through appreciation of the habit can sometime undermine it. Which makes tillexophobia almost inevitable. It's like a cramp or a tic, but don't worry. More often than not it resolves on its own. I'm sure Professor Fawck will be interested in the data you've produced today, but in my view, there's nothing one can say of it until we scan you again. If you don't mind, I'd like to see you again in a couple of months."

---

296   Linchak, Mickey. "Nosepicking as Dissociation" *Lacan Journal* Vol. 247 (May 2011) 27–35.

EIGHTEEN

I called Fawck and made an appointment for later that day, then headed for lunch in the student cafeteria. While I ate, I checked my email. I wasn't altogether surprised to find that Mickey had sent his article from the *Lacan Journal* which Klondyke had just mentioned to me. There was also a message from Sara and messages, with attached research, from Joe Johnson and Ann Curtis. Sara wrote that she'd obtained the application for the Templeton nomination and directed her staff to gather the information it required. She'd also called George's friend, the IRS director, who'd promised to email an application for our tax exemption, and she'd spoken with one of Murgate's lawyers about setting up the foundation it would require. Ann Curtis sent more work on idio-picking, Joe Johnson an extensive collection of blog-response to George's vlog. I scanned all this quickly, then turned to Mickey's article. A couple of lines was all I needed to understand why he'd not, as with most of his published work, sent it to me before it was printed. His anti-nasalism was now unequivocal.

"One cannot avoid the conclusion that nose-picking mitigates anxiety and is thus, at root, nothing more than a form of escape and self-denial. Call it masturbation, call it neurosis. It amounts to the same thing. Furthermore, it doesn't work unless it occurs in a state of dissociation. Awareness of its utility will make it ineffective. Let us say that the hand that picks must do so behind the picker's back."[297]

I sent him a note, suggesting we meet to talk about the article, then forwarded it to Carlotta so she'd file it for me. Finished with lunch, I looked at the news and, looking toward my next blog, made some notes on the morning's events. As every day since he'd gone missing, I sent a note to George and begged him to get in touch with me. I was about to close my laptop when a message from Klondyke arrived. He'd sent three articles on tillexophobia, the video file of my scan, a summary of the data he'd collected while I was in the chair, and, as promised, the work from Prague on "secondary product." Once again, he entreated me to come back in a couple of months "so we can have another look."

Fawck's office was just three floors above the cafeteria. I paused outside his door to make sure my phone was on. I also checked its audio file. Empty. Which meant, of course, that everything I'd recorded, in the lab and in Klondyke's office, was not only safe in my own, Carlotta's, and Sara's mailboxes, but already transcribed on their word processors.[298]

Fawck greeted me warmly, taking my hand in both of his. He was a large man with a barrel chest, a trimmed white Hemingway beard and a surprisingly high-pitched voice that seemed to come entirely from his throat. He had bushy white eyebrows and large, sad blue eyes fixed in a state of what seemed to be consternation. His office was small and dark, more than a little incommodious, I thought, for a man of his stature, but as more than one of his biographers notes, he'd several times refused the administration's offer of more

---

297   Ibid.

298   Indeed, as she'd later write in her memoir (Martinson, op. cit., 325), she was reading the transcript at the very moment when I was sitting down at Fawck's desk.

comfortable quarters. The only decoration was a quote, in German, from Emmanuel Kant – "The hand is the window of the mind" (**Figure 17**) – and a small reproduction of Kruger's *Your Nose is a Battleground*, which I'd seen earlier on a bus advertisement. The ceiling was low and cracked, the furniture the sort you see on sidewalks outside stores selling used office equipment – grey metal desk, two straight metal chairs, a single tacky modernistic desk lamp, and a green billiard light hanging from the ceiling on a silver metal chain gone dark with tarnish. No rug, no fax or answering machine, no pictures or diplomas on the wall, not a single book in sight. His laptop – wirelessly linked, I knew, to the university's mainframe and the large flat-screen monitor on the wall – sat alone on his desk. His work-surface was otherwise bare except for a bottle of liquid Rhinobate and a box of facial tissues.

Figure 17   Emmanuel Kant quote.

"Tissues?" I said.

"Why not? I blow when I need to these days. Don't you?"

"Sometimes."

"Not always?"

"When I need to," I repeated. "Why the Rhinobate?"

"You know why."

"No, I don't."

"Well, you should."

He opened a desk drawer, removed a syringe, and filled it with Rhinobate. From the same drawer he removed a black strap, wrapped it around his left bicep, and tapped to find a vein. Finally, he injected himself. "Not picking is a muscle," he said. "You have to develop it the way you develop arms and legs with weight-training. It's easy not to pick when you don't have a crust. It's when you do that the work begins. Rhinobate is weight-training. I take it so as not to pick the crusts that it creates."

I stretched my arm across his desk. "Can I join you?"

Refilling the syringed, he removed the strap from his arm, wrapped it around mine, found a vein, and injected me as he'd injected himself.

"Thanks," I said.

He squeezed the tissue around his nose, blew hard, and then, spreading it on his desk, leaned close to examine his discharge. Of course he was well aware of the Czechoslovakian mucus research which Klondyke had just sent me.[299] I saw him squinting. "Waiting alters mucus," he explained. "Have you noticed? Day by day, I see my liquidity increasing." He wadded the tissue and dropped it in a waste basket under his desk. Then he moved to the edge of his chair and straightened his back impressively. "Klondyke emailed your scan to me. Let's have a look at it."

He tapped a string of commands on his keyboard. A moment later, my scan appeared on his wall-monitor. "He calls you tillexophobic? Absurd. You're not the least afraid to pick." He pursed his lips and stared into my eyes. "I call you PostNasal. I've got seventeen scans like yours on my hard drive. My own makes eighteen. I scan myself at least once a week. In other words, we've got eighteen brains that aren't completely at the mercy of discomfort. I'd wager anything that your scan looks like the others."

At first glance, the image on his monitor looked like the beautiful, multicolored abstractions – CAT scans, PET scans,

---

299   Drobny, Jaroslav. Drobny34.com. As Klondyke had noted, Drobny was no lightweight. His work would show a definitive relationship between sinus fluid and neurotransmitter uptake receptors, specifically serotonin and noradrenalin.

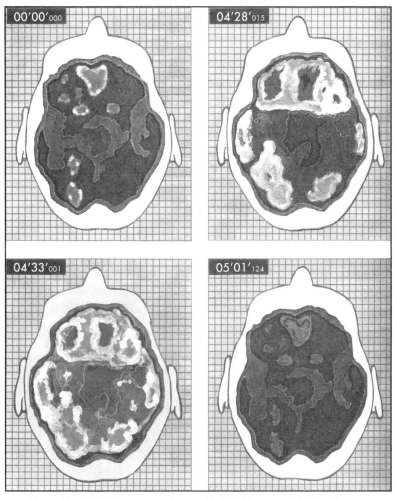

Figure 18 Illustration accompanying Fawck's first Rhinomag article. *Scientific American*, June 2010.

        (a) resting brain: 00'00'000
        (b) initial crust sensation: 04'28'015
        (c) initial insertion: 04'33'001
        (d) crust-membrane separation – twinge: 05'01'124

MRIs, etc. – we're used to seeing on TV documentaries (**Figure 18**). The Rhinomag, however, was a lot more advanced than the scanners that used to produce those images. First- and second-generation imaging machines were basically still cameras, but the one which Fawck and Klondyke used was a so-called "4D Scanner" which captured changes in blood flow at the instant they occurred. The result was moving images of the brain in process. In the upper left-hand corner of the initial image on the monitor was a digital clock which registered thousandths of a second.[300] Beginning when the scanner switched on, seconds after the cone had been lowered and the collar tightened on my head, a little over four minutes after my Rhinobate injection, it showed 00'00'000, but Fawck advanced it quickly to the moment – 04'28'015 – when I'd first felt bilateral irritation. He had a trackball mouse he operated with his forefinger, clicking on commands in the toolbar to zoom in or out, advance the scan, or, as now, trace a circle with his cursor around a small cluster of cells near the center of the screen.

His voice was reverential. "The nasal cortex."

With more keystrokes, he zoomed in, enlarging the image until the cluster he'd encircled (somewhere between .005 and .006 mm in diameter, according to data which was itself, of course, immediately available by means of a right-click) filled the screen entirely. "In other words," he went on, "the dorsal cells of the frontal insula. Here's first awareness. See? Rhinobate hits you, boom, in both nostrils. The trigeminal impulse is bilateral, but the initial perception is here, in these neurons. We've seen an explosion in insula research in the last few years. Finally, it's here that attraction and repulsion originate, all the excitement you describe in the first of your wonderful blogs. This is what precedes discomfort – the distinction between

---

300 Needless to say, the Rhinomag was capable of finer temporal distinctions, its clock capable of displaying millions or even trillions of a second. Recent versions of the scanner are said to be thousands of times more sensitive.

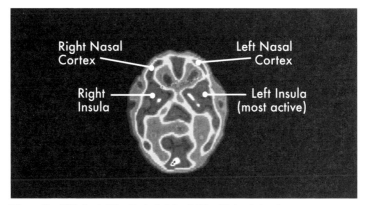

Figure 19 *Right Insula/Nasal Lobe. Left Insula/Nasal Lobe. Activated.*

A bilateral view of the frontal insula, which rhinologists, taking their cue from Robert Fawck, call "the Nasal Cortex." The insula itself is a prune-sized region under the frontal lobes that is thought to register gut feeling and play a critical role in addictive behavior. Recent research suggests, for example, that smokers whose insula are damaged by stroke are up to 136 times more likely to undergo a disruption of their addiction than smokers without such damage. The insula of PostNasalists, who practice patience and thus (to use Fawck's terminology) "transcend" their addiction to nose-picking, have been found to be metabolically similar to those of stroke patients, as well as smaller and less dense than Nasalists, who pick with abandon. Such data has fueled the fires of the Nasalist-PostNasalist conflict, encouraging those, like Jamie Morales, who maintains that "patience is nothing more than a euphemism for repression," not to mention Fawck-haters like neurologist Edwina Charlemane, who once (on FOX "Sunday Morning Medicine," April 16, 2013) used the aforementioned data to support her belief that "PostNasalism is a form of brain damage."

comfort and discomfort. Some have called this cluster of cells the discrimination lobe. Likes and dislikes, the craving to pursue the one or avoid the other – it's in these cells that such polarity begins. It's also here that a lot of signals from the body are received, processed, and then relayed or, as we say, broadcast to other circuits. Later today I'll email you a bunch of insula stuff. If it doesn't blow your mind it's only because you haven't understood it." Once again, he circled the area with his cursor. The target cells were highly activated, bright yellow at this instant, much more intense in their illumination than those adjacent to it. "Your nasal cortex," he said again. "The root of picking and the concentration and simplification that you describe, in my opinion, better than anyone else." Summarizing the rhinological research and using his cursor to direct my eyes, he repeated much of what I'd learned already from my studies of the work he'd done with Klondyke and the file Carlotta had emailed. He advanced the scan second by second. "Once these cells get activated, excitation spreads rapidly through the frontal lobes, the temporal lobes, and the cerebellum. See this here? And here? All of it originates in the nasal cortex and, before that, crust-irritation, bang-bang shots from the trigeminal nerve. Our data indicates that these cells, here, in the frontal lobe, are activated .0034 nanoseconds after the nasal cortex. And these here, in the temporal lobe, .0041. The frontal lobe generates the need to pick and the temporal the concentration that makes it so exciting. And obviously, the need to extract becomes more and more consuming the more the excitation spreads. For the next five to eight minutes, there's nothing in your brain but this need. See this here? And here? That's the root of it! The excitation from a single crust permeates the whole of the cortical brain! Look at the motor cortex! The prefrontal cortex! These are areas that regulate emotional output, and these here have been shown to regulate self-control. All are working in concert to activate your fingertip! You know the feeling: Go for it! Get rid of it!"

All this, of course, was elementary Nasalism, the principal theme and drama of Klondyke's book. For Fawck, however, as he demonstrated now, it was just the beginning. As he'd written in one of the blogs Carlotta had forwarded, "The conventional rhinotillexic paradigm is kindergarten Nasalism."[301] Now, to my surprise, he reversed the scan, running it back 3.086 seconds to the instant he'd circled the nasal cortex with his cursor. "We call this moment 'desire origination.'" Circling another cluster of cells with his cursor, he explained, "This is the frontal amygdala.

301   Fawck, Robert. Rfawck.com, April 16, 2009.

This small cluster of cells is where the desire to extract is born. Its activation follows activation of the insula by less than .002 nanoseconds. We call this the craving lobe. It's where desire begins and it's also, obviously, the source of the feelings, like discontent and disappointment, which flood our brains when desire is frustrated.

"If you study the scans of quick-pickers, you'll see that the craving lobe and the nasal cortex will pretty much drive their habit. Freedom from crusts is not just what they want. It's *all* they want! The whole of the brain is mobilized behind this single, intense desire. But at a certain point, the equation is reversed. You won't see the reversal on PostNasal scans like yours or mine, but on quick-pick scans it's unequivocal. Here – I'll show you one."

His fingers worked his keyboard again. With a few keystrokes, he split the screen and, with a few more, he brought up another scan next to my own. "Here's an obsessive habit. Exuberant, unapologetic. Big crust right now. Bothering him a lot. See the trigeminal activation? The motor neurons? His fingertip is already activated! It's always the same. Activated insula, activated craving lobe… and now… look! The whole of the cortex! This is concentration! Desire! At this moment, there's nothing but crust in this guy's head. This is the peak of Nasalism, the epiphany. But wait a minute! Watch what happens now!"

He advanced the scan even more slowly than he had before – a thousandth of a second at a time. "What Klondyke doesn't understand is that, in the final analysis, nose-picking is an *ironic experience*. When extraction occurs, the craving lobe deactivates! Desire is one thing, desire fulfilled, another. When you get your crust, your craving lobe deactivates! Why is this so? Klondyke doesn't get this. This is why he sends his PostNasalists to me. Nothing is so uncomfortable as an activated craving lobe! The goal of all desire is not the object toward which it's pointed but freedom from desire itself. Here, I'll show you."

Once again he advanced the scan. "What's going on? Extraction, right? He got it! Feels the twinge… see that flash? Withdraws his finger. Bingo! You know the feeling. It's like he won the lottery. What's going on now? What do you see?"

"The color's fading."

"Exactly. Desire fulfilled produces cortical deactivation. As neurons deactivate, they lose intensity of color until, as you see now, they're altogether colorless. Finally, the scan goes white! Deactivation spreads! Temporal lobe! Frontal lobe! Cerebellum! Finally – see this? and this? – we've got global deactivation! Freedom from the brain! This is the joy of extraction. You set a goal and achieve it, and for a moment or two, you're free of your brain."

Fawck shifted in his chair as I was shifting in mine. Less than ten minutes had passed since we'd injected Rhinobate, but it was beginning to take effect. He was sniffing loudly, his nostrils twitching as they always do when irritated, and I was raising and lowering my upper lip and, now and again, shifting my nose from side to side as if to scratch one nostril with the other. Even as we did so, however, our eyes were fixed on his monitor.

His finger caressed the wheel of his mouse as his cursor raced around the screen. "For Klondyke, this epiphany is the bottom line, the motivation and justification. Discomfort, desire, concentration, relief. I don't put him down for that. He's sincere about this work and sincere about his practice. But why is he so fucking conservative? Why can't he acknowledge Post Extraction Despair? Guys like us, we face it down. No one has crusts all the time! What do we do in between them? The guy you just saw – doesn't he want another epiphany? Bet your ass he does! Show me anyone on earth who can have the experience he just had without wanting it again. Watch him now!"

Again he advanced the scan slowly. "What do you see?"

"Color again. Spreading."

"Right. The deactivation lasted, what, ten seconds? Eleven?

His brain is busy again! Look at these language cells. He's thinking! Making plans! No more contentment. No more silence for sure. This is PED! Like a baby wants his mother's tit, he wants another crust! In the end, Nasalism leads to more Nasalism. The more you pick, the more you need to. Where's the freedom in that?"

Pausing again, he leaned back in his chair and squeezed his nose with what seemed a kind of ferocity. The effects of Rhinobate were more and more apparent for both of us. His nose was shifting from side to side and mine felt entirely blocked.

"Yeah, for Klondyke that's the whole story. But once you get to PED, you ask a different question. I ask it, anyway. *You* ask it. Even if we've not completely rejected extraction, we're no longer slaves to it. Forced to wait, goddamn it, we begin to… *investigate waiting*. You know what that means! Patience! Time stretches out. You're not after immediate gratification anymore. You're thinking long term. A taste of patience is a taste of freedom from the brain."

He advanced the scan rapidly, moving his cursor with random, jagged, almost doodling movement so that it looked like an insect on the screen. Wrinkling his nose again, he rubbed it very hard with the back of his hand.

"It's true extraction frees you from your brain, but how long does such freedom last? Eleven seconds? Twelve? Some people are satisfied with such relief but not PostNasalists. Not you and me. We want more! Freedom from the brain is sanity. A few seconds isn't enough for us. Ordinary pickers, extraction leaves them more depressed than before. You and me, we're done with depression. And that means – done with crusts! We're tired of being tyrannized by them. We want sanity!"

My crusts were fully developed now, typically aggressive, but I was calm in relation to them. It was almost as if the irritation they produced were happening outside me.

Rubbing his nose again, Fawck entered more commands from his keyboard. The tillexic scan disappeared from the screen, leaving mine to fill the whole of it again.

"No need to repeat the whole melodrama. Let's start right here with crust maturity. You've been through it a thousand times. Nasal irritation, trigeminal activation. Total discomfort. Crusts alive and screaming, pressing against the septum. You're dying to pick but wait… what's this? No activation of the fingertip? No extraction? Where do we go from here?"

Again, he advanced the scan. "What do you see now?"

Though I knew what was coming, I have to say that what I saw filled me with emotion. Whiteness proliferated. Color drained from one area after another (**Figure 20**).

"This is grace," he said, "a state beyond description. Words insult it! Patience is brain deactivation, and brain deactivation is silence. All because you do not pick! Because you're patient! You aren't thinking, aren't even conscious. Look at your language cells! Your insula! For once in your life, you're completely sane!"

"But what produces that? Where in the brain does patience come from?"

"Nowhere!" he cried. "That's the beauty of it. The brain cannot deactivate itself! It has to come from… somewhere else!"

He rubbed his nose again, pinching it hard, closing his eyes as if in pain. I noticed that I was inhaling and exhaling with unusual force and making a lot of noise as I did so.

Fawck went on. "The ultimate question a PostNasalist asks is 'what do I want most?' Short-term or long-term gratification. Extraction of a single crust or freedom from my brain?"

He was sniffing more often now. Again and again, his nostrils made the whistling sound the breath produces when it has to circumnavigate a crust. His finger was nervous on his trackball, the movement of his cursor random and chaotic. My scan had

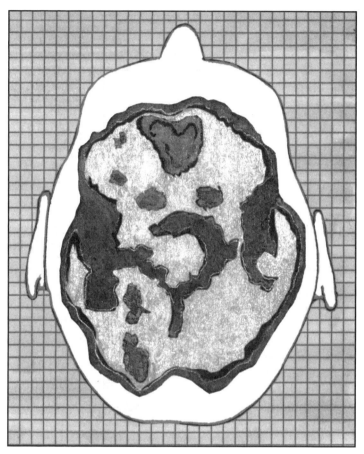

Figure 20 *The patient brain. White male, age 34, no extraction 31 months.*

At this moment, not-picking what will turn out to be an 8.3. The state of global neurological deactivation which Fawck calls "the ultimate long-term gratification of PostNasalism." The enduring effects of patience have been shown to diminish the size and density of the frontal insula and, some maintain, the insula in general. Indeed, pathologist Harcourt Thomas of Rockefeller University claims that PostNasal neocortexes are the smallest and thinnest of any he's ever found on autopsy. Needless to say, those like Edwina Charlemagne who call PostNasalism brain damage or even, like Perle McIntire of Oral Roberts University, "nasalobotomy" find confirmation of their point of view in images such as this. Interviewed with McIntire on Charlie Rose (October 18, 2013), Fawck's rejoinder, when she summarized her views about PostNasalism and lobotomy, was that she suffered from "a terminal case of impatience."

just reached twelve minutes when he leaned back in his chair, placed his right fist, fiercely clinched, at the bottom of his nostrils, and then, to my astonishment, inserted his forefinger.

"What are you doing?" I cried.

Pushing higher, he did not reply. His eyes were closed, his brow furrowed. I was stunned. "But... you're totally contradicting everything you've said!"

Turning, active, his finger went deeper, but even so, he nodded. "You're right!" he cried. "I do it again and again!"

A long silence ensued while he picked with abandon. As usual with rhinobatoids, this meant both nostrils, two to three minutes which totally absorbed him. His face was quiet and withdrawn and, of course, familiar, the mix of contentment and excitement which all of us know and yearn for.

Finished, he wiped his fingers and dropped his tissue in the waste basket. Splayed and slightly arched, not unlike a pianist's, his fingers rested on his keyboard again. For several minutes, he was silent, not a little stunned, I thought, shaking his head with a kind of amazement and idly tapping keys so as to cause a rapid fire string of disconnected letters on his screen. "Yes," he sighed. "Again and again. As if the body has a will of its own. Patience deactivates the insula but, if it's not complete, the motor cells can overcome it. Sometimes I think there's an inverse relationship between these two regions. As if deactivation of the insula produces even more activity in the motor cells. You saw it, right? That wasn't ordinary picking. My finger was fierce! How can I be anything but forgiving toward myself? Show me anyone who can keep his finger still when his motor cells are firing like that! If anything, patience seems to excite them more!"

Thanks to my recorder/cell phone, which was faithfully transmitting our conversation to Sara's computer and, by voice recognition software, to her word processor, which would make it possible for me to include it in the blog I wrote a few days later as well as in the last chapter of *The Complete Book of Nasalism*, most of my readers probably know what I said now. Some have celebrated it as "the first summation" or "the ultimate apology" for PostNasalism, but others have called it "an attack on thought itself" or even, to quote the blogger, Nopick, who is said to be the most prominent anti-nasal voice on the web,[302] "a celebration of lobotomy."[303] In any event, produced as they were by the Founder with what seemed to be the absolute non-participation of my brain, it's difficult to believe that anyone could have been more surprised by them than I was myself.

"You saw the scan. Patience is freedom from discrimination. What's contradiction to a brain in this condition? There's no difference between anything and whatever you used to call its opposite. Logic? Consistency? Understanding? How can you miss them? They don't exist anymore! You said it yourself. Patience is freedom from the brain. The only sanity you'll ever know!"[304]

Silent, he shook his head in agreement.

"And what about your crusts? Will you ignore them altogether?"

"Hardly," I said.

I reached across the desk, took a tissue from the box and blew into it vigorously.

"Thank you," he said.

---

302 *Newsweek* April 18, 2011; Salon.com, March 30, 2011; *The New Yorker* June 5, 2011.

303 Nopick.com, September 19, 2011.

304 Linchak, Walker. Wlinchak.com, May 12, 2011; Linchak, *The Complete Book of Nasalism*, op. cit., 1296.

NINETEEN

I left his office late in the evening. Traffic was heavy, the trip to the airport very slow and halting and – until I asked the driver to turn off his radio and silenced the video screen in the back seat, which continued, in silence, to display news updates, weather reports, and a stock-ticker as well as offering, according to a banner on the left side, an array of entertainment that included several prime-time TV shows, YouTube, and a couple of videogames – claustrophobic. Fortunately, Wi-Fi was everywhere available, my wireless connection uninterrupted all the way to the airport, so I was able to get some work done.

The first thing I saw when I booted was an IM from Sara.

"Bullshit"

"Who"

"Fawck"

"And me?"

"Worse"

On the video screen, the headlines traced the Guatemala mudslide (350 estimated dead now), spreading fires in California, a typhoon in Bangladesh, and, of course, the continuing saga of George's disappearance. There was still no sign of him, but on blogs, websites, and the whole spectrum of Internet news, rumors about his situation constantly evolved. Among the latest were reports of him working on a farm in Iraq, living with

Osama Bin Laden in the Tora Bora region of Afghanistan, hospitalized again in Dallas, and dead by suicide. Most of these tales, of course, were accompanied by photographs, video streams, or personal accounts which claimed to verify them. As I followed them now, a bulletin announced that he'd been kidnapped off his Texas ranch by "terrorists of unknown nationality." There was a picture of a man his size, sitting in a straight-backed metal chair, face covered by a black hood, guarded by two men or women wearing similar hoods and armed with submachine guns.

I turned off the video screen and went online again. With all the email I had waiting, traffic became irrelevant. I had Klondyke's message, with my scan attached, and messages, with attachments, from Joe Johnson and Alan Fortas. Joe had sent research on the anterior cingulate cortex, an emotional center of the brain that, according to its author, "is aroused when a person feels compelled to act in two different ways but must choose between them." Interesting though it was, Joe's email was trumped by Alan's. God knows why, but he was the first of my staff to investigate translation websites. How was it possible we'd waited so long to find rhinotillexis in German (*Nase-Auswahl*), French (*le nez choisit*), and Italian (*raccolto del naso*)?[305] There wasn't time for in-depth research, of course, but quick searches in each language produced thousands of hits each time. I'd just searched *nez choisit* when another IM from Sara arrived.

"Fuck you"

"Again?"

"Check your email."

Her message had three attachments. The first – thanks, as I've noted, to voice-recognition software – was the whole of

---

305 Soon he'd send me Dutch and Portuguese. He'd also located Chinese, Japanese, Korean, Greek, and Russian, but only in their script. It would be several days before we transliterated it.

my conversation with Fawck. The others were copies of notes between them – her request and his consent for permission to publish our conversation in the next issue of *MurgateLive*.

Traffic froze in gridlock, moved a bit, then froze again. Horns honked all around us. I forwarded the Fawck transcript to Carlotta and then, on impulse, shot George an email. "Tell me at least if you're alive."

I opened Joe's message. "I thought this might be of use to you." Attached was an old article from *The Journal of Neuroscience*.

AREA RESPONSIBLE FOR 'SELF-CONTROL' FOUND IN THE HUMAN BRAIN; MAY HELP EXPLAIN WHY SOME PEOPLE ARE IMPULSIVE

WASHINGTON, DC – The area of the brain responsible for self-control – where the decision *not* to do something occurs after thinking about doing it – is separate from the area associated with taking action.

"The results illuminate a very important aspect of the brain's control of behavior, the ability to hold off doing something after you've developed the intention to do it – one might call it 'free won't' as opposed to free will," says Martha Farah, PhD, of the University of Pennsylvania. "It is very important to identify the circuits that enable 'free won't' because of the many psychiatric disorders for which self-control problems figure prominently – from Attention-Deficit Disorder to substance dependence and various personality disorders." Farah was not involved in the experiment.

The findings broaden understanding of the neural basis for decision making, or free will, and may help explain why some individuals are impulsive while others are reluctant to act, says lead author Marcel Brass, PhD, of the Max Planck Institute for Human Cognitive and Brain Sciences and Ghent University. Brass and Patrick Haggard, PhD, of University College London, used functional magnetic resonance imaging (fMRI) to study the brain activity of participants pressing a button at times they chose themselves. They compared data from these trials to results when the participants prepared to hit the button, then decided to hold back or veto the action.

Fifteen right-handed participants were asked to press a button on a keyboard. They were asked to choose some cases in which they stopped just before pressing the button. Participants also indicated on a clock the time at which they intended to press the button or decided to hold back. When Brass and Haggard compared fMRI images of the two scenarios, they found that pulling back yielded activity in the dorsal fronto-median cortex (dFMC), an area on the midline of the brain directly above the eyes, which did not show up when participants followed through and made the action. In addition, those who chose to stop the intended action most often showed greatest contrast in dFMC activity.

"The capacity to withhold an action that we have prepared but reconsidered is an important distinction between intelligent and impulsive behavior," says Brass, "and also between humans and other animals."

✺ ✺ ✺ ✺

The cabbie was on his cell phone, talking into the air in a language I could not understand. He steered with his left hand and gesticulated with his right. I opened Klondyke's message and inserted the video of my scan into the transcript of my conversation with Fawck. Thus, I could now review his explanation of nasalneurology with the added benefit of the images he'd used to illustrate it. I read it twice with extreme discomfort that, like most discomfort I'd felt recently, did not bother me in the least. I could not deny that he seemed irrational, even pathological, but in comparison, I thought, to what?

Another IM from Sara. "Got it!"

I answered her as traffic cleared and the taxi moved again.

Figure 21 Image of ex-President George W. Bush, guarded by terrorists, which appeared after his disappearance. Though soon discredited, it can still be viewed on YouTube as well as fraudulent blogs and websites – Alqaeda.com, Skinhead.com, Nopick.com, et al – which claim to represent terrorist groups which orchestrated the kidnapping. It appears on the cover of *Terrorism, A History* (San Francisco: Harper-Collins, 2013) and in the *Bush and Nasalism* DVD, published in 2012 by Murgate Entertainment.

"???"

"Fawck is right. The body has a will of its own. All this talk – patience, non-discrimination – intellectual! And you? As usual, living in your mind. Denying concrete reality."

"Mind? Body? Why discriminate between them?"

"Because I'm a human being"

"And me?"

"Your guess good as mine"

A few minutes later, the cab pulled into the airport. We wound our way through the feeder roads and finally entered the departure lane. On the video screen, I saw the picture of George and his captors again. I was about to close my laptop when his IM appeared. "Alive? Oh yeah. Unfortunately."

"Thank God," I replied, and then, on impulse again, "Check your email." I attached the transcript of my conversation with Fawck and sent it off to him.

Late for the shuttle, I ran to the gate but arrived just after the doors had closed. With an hour to kill, I took a seat in the waiting room. The light was good and I wanted to work, but across from me and to my left and right were people on cell phones. Two seats down, a teenager had rock on his boom box, and overhead, volume so loud one couldn't ignore it, the TV showed CNN. The same weatherwoman I'd seen earlier was reciting and pointing to the radar map. Headlines above the stock ticker at the bottom of the screen showed the Guatemalan toll over 500. The California fires had forced more than 200,000 to evacuate, and the typhoon toll was over 5,000. As for George, there was increasing speculation that his kidnappers were American. Angry NeoCons, according to one blog, Christian Fundamentalists, according to another. I opened my laptop, went online through the wireless connection in the airport, and Googled "Bush Kidnapped." First among the thousands of hits was a YouTube video of his beheading. The swift, terrible image of slashing sword and falling head was one I'd often seen before, of course, but I'd never seen one so convincing. One could not doubt that the face one saw when the hood came off belonged to George W. Bush.

I sent it to him with a message: "You call this alive?"

His IM came at once. "Sad to say it's fake."

Sara IMed again. "Impatience = spontaneous. Patience = rigidity, repression."

I stared at their messages for a moment, then sent the same answer to both. "???"

New York weather was on the screen overhead. Rain. Checking my email, I found a message from Carlotta. Inspired by my dialogue with Fawck, she'd Googled *patience*. There was research – attached in full, of course, but mercifully summarized by her – from Korea, Argentina, and the University of Tennessee.[306] The first indicated connection to "hippocampal thickness," the second to "Limbic activation-patterns," and the third to fluctuations of serotonin and noradrenalin.

Sara continued as my plane was announced. "Finally, it's about time, no? Picking = now. Patience = future. In other words, spontaneity again. Why do I need patience? All my life I've been outside the present."

First to board, I found a bulkhead seat again. Settling in, I arranged my laptop on the meal tray, connected my headset, adjusted the screens in my spectacles, and opened my word processor. Any writer will understand the yearning I felt now. My head was spinning with all the information I'd processed these last twelve hours. I needed to organize it, shape it into a blog. Already, I could taste the calm and confidence I'd always found in doing so. To my amazement, however, I found my mind empty of language, my memory a blank.

I waited, stared at the screen for a moment, then all at once, to my amazement, typed a single line dictated by the Founder. I never uploaded it and never included it in a blog, but two years later, as you may know, it would conclude my acceptance speech at the Templeton Award ceremony.[307]

"Patience is God."

---

306   Linchak, *The Complete Book of Nasalism*, op. cit., Appendix 6.

307   See the video stream on Templeton.org. It may also be heard on NPR.com or WBAI.com. Video streams of the argument generated by this speech may be seen on Foxnews.com, CNN.com, BillMoyers.com, and, in broad parody, Thedailyshow.com. Needless to say, all are available on YouTube.

I copied it into an email which I sent to Sara and George. Then I removed my headset. The plane had just backed out of the gate. The seat beside me had been taken by a teenage girl. She was small and thin, with a sad narrow face, dark eyes with darker bags beneath them, a streak of purple henna in her blond hair, two studs in the ear and one in the nostril on my side. She wore green cargo pants, a red Harvard sweatshirt, and earbuds linked, I figured, by wireless magic to the iPhone gripped in her tiny hand. Settling in beside me, she placed it on her meal tray and tapped a series of buttons. While the plane moved slowly over the tarmac, she surfed from website to website until she found her way to YouTube and brought up Bush on "Larry King Live."

Sara's IM did not surprise me. "Fuck you."

"Again, again?"

"Answer me, dammit."

"I did."

"No U didn't."

"U weren't listening."

The pilot announced that we were cleared for take-off. As the plane made its turn and accelerated, an IM from George appeared. "Fucking brilliant, you and Fawck both. My thoughts exactly." Removing my headset, I watched the landscape rushing past my window and, a moment later, falling away below. When we'd reached our cruising altitude, I found he'd continued.

"Impatience ruined my life! All my arrogance – impatience! All my childishness – impatience! Iraq, Katrina, Global Warming. What was in my head? I didn't know how to stop and think."

The plane hit turbulence, bumping hard, three times in succession. In the past, I'd always been frightened by this sort of thing, but I noticed, to my amazement, that it didn't bother me in the least.

"Where are you?" I wrote.

"Hiding out."

"From what?"

"Myself. My life. My mistakes."

"Hiding is picking."

"What else can you do when you don't have the guts to kill yourself?"

"Suicide is picking."

"Yeah? Well, some boogers can't be ignored."

I took off my headset and dozed a while. When the pilot announced that we'd soon be landing in New York, I put it on again and found another IM from Sara.

"Google *impatience*."

TWENTY

She was sleeping when I got home. Naked, warm, wrapping her arms around me, whispering "Hi" when I climbed into bed beside her, stripping my mind of information the moment my head touched the pillow.

Next morning, waking first, I made coffee while she slept. By the time it was ready, she'd awakened as well. Returning to the kitchen, I poured each of us a cup and, upon my return, found her sniffing Rhinobate from the back of her hand. As I climbed into bed beside her, she tapped out another dose and offered her hand to me. I inhaled deeply through each nostril. Here it was again, my nostrils awake with pungency and heat, my brain with anticipation and suspense. Sipping our coffee, we awaited our rhinobatoids in silence. A few minutes later, just as I felt the first swelling in my right nostril, her left hand rose to her nose, then paused as if suspended at the tip.

"Coming with me?" she said.

"No," I said.

Her finger did not move. "Please."

"No."

"Wally, please."

"No," I said again.

She leaned toward her night-table, opened the drawer, and removed a small pistol with a pearl handle and a short barrel.

I'd never seen it before. This was a woman who'd published books and articles attacking the NRA, who'd marched once in Washington to support anti-gun laws.

"Don't make me ask you again."

"You're kidding."

She shifted the gun to her right hand and put the barrel against my head. "Don't underestimate me."

"Stop it, Sara. Don't fuck around."

She tapped the barrel twice against my temple. "So hard it's always been for you to take me at my word. What is this but respect for what you taught me? If I let you back off, I betray you, betray the practice, reject everything we've found together."

Her finger rose to her nose again, entering this time. "You gave me this!" she cried. "Made me understand it! I used to think it was just a bad habit. Just picking! You made me see it's freedom! Self-expression! Honesty! Do this, you're true to yourself. Hold back, you're living a lie! No, don't shake your head! I won't let you trivialize it." Her finger turned, pushing higher. "This is truth! Meaning! Clarity and peace! It's why we read, why we study, why we write. How can you reject it? Turn against this and you turn against your work! I can't let you do this to yourself! I respect you too much!"

I shook my head. "You'll never pull that trigger. You need me to do the book."

"Where's the book if you turn against picking?"

"You're over the top, Sara. You sound like a Fundamentalist."

She pressed the gun against my head. "In other words, not a good girl anymore. Thanks to you. Standing up at last for what I believe."

Shrill and thin, my voice betrayed more fear than I thought I felt. "You're a monster!"

"No," she said, "a human being."

I laughed. "Is there any difference?"

I half expected she'd laugh with me, but as you know from her memoir,[308] I could not have been more wrong.

"Laugh once more," she said, "and I swear to God I'll pull the trigger."

Frightened though I was, I could not restrain myself. Exploding as if independent of me, my laughter filled the room.

She was true to her word. The click of the trigger was loud in my ear. "Bang!" she cried, laughing with me.

---

308 Martinson, op. cit.

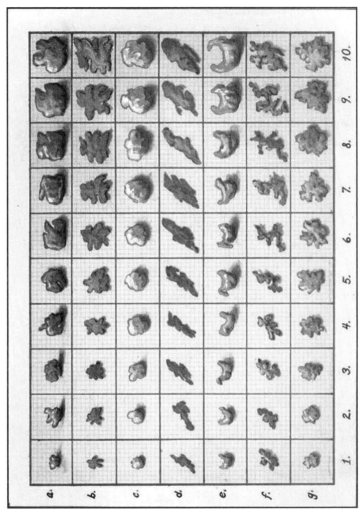

Figure 22 *Bloch Classification scale*

Early version of Lucille Bloch's crust classification scale. While its oversimplifications are acknowledged by most rhinologists, including Bloch herself, its historical value remains unquestioned. "Its greatest shortcoming," Bloch admits, "is its underestimation of adhesion and tenacity. In other words, its naive equation of volume and density with extraction and twinge." Later versions of this scale, emphasizing what Bloch calls "extraction experience," are less visual or, to quote her again, "less materialistic."

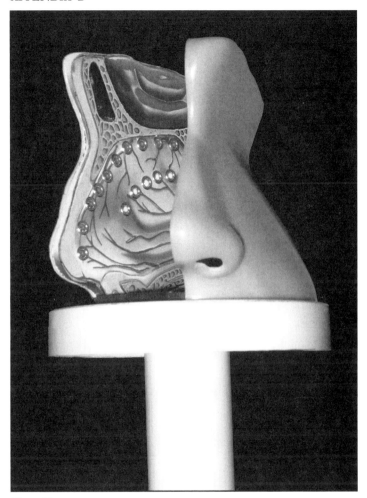

Figure 23
    Nose Model developed by Marcus Klondyke and Brazilian sculptor, Manuel Olivados; software by Harriet Van Pelt and MicroSoft. The original is owned by the Murgate Institute of Rhinology, Pasadena, California. Currently on loan to the Metropolitan Museum, New York City, where it is displayed in the sculpture garden.

ACKNOWLEDGEMENT

As most writers know, books don't get written without the support, good will, and patience of others, and I can't believe there's anyone more fortunate than I in this regard. For help with illustration and design, I am grateful to Michael Flanagan, Georgiana Goodwin, and Rose Unes; for near heroic editorial assistance, Eliza Jane Wood; for careful, critical reading, Rudy Wurlitzer, Michael Flanagan again, Steven Shainberg, Andra Samelson, and my agent, Jane Gelfman. Finally, for patience far beyond the call of duty, my wife, Vivian Bower.